TO WIN A VISCOUNT'S HEART

The Rakes of Mayhem
Book 5

Anna St. Claire

ARE YOU SIGNED UP FOR DRAGONBLADE'S BLOG?

You'll get the latest news and information on exclusive giveaways, exclusive excerpts, coming releases, sales, free books, cover reveals and more.

Check out our complete list of authors, too!

No spam, no junk. That's a promise!

Sign Up Here

www.dragonbladepublishing.com

Dearest Reader;

Thank you for your support of a small press. At Dragonblade Publishing, we strive to bring you the highest quality Historical Romance from some of the best authors in the business. Without your support, there is no 'us', so we sincerely hope you adore these stories and find some new favorite authors along the way.

Happy Reading!

CEO, Dragonblade Publishing

Additional Dragonblade books by Author Anna St. Claire

The Rakes of Mayhem Series
The Earl of Excess (Book 1)
The Marquess of Mischief (Book 2)
The Duke of Disorder (Book 3)
The Baron's Return (Book 4)
To Win a Viscount's Heart (Book 5)
A Gift for Agatha (Novella)

The Lyon's Den Series
Lyon's Prey
The Heart of a Lyon
Once Upon a Winter's Tale (Novella)
A Lyon of Her Own

Also from Anna St. Claire
Once upon a Haunted Heart (Novella)

PROLOGUE

Grosvenor Square, Mayfair
London, England
June 1813

"Kiss me," the lady demanded in a seductive tone. "No one will see us here."

"I aim to please, my lady," Gerald Lawrence said huskily, stepping into the jasmine-covered gazebo at the end of the garden path.

He took her into his arms, and his lips skimmed hers as he took measure of the low-cut red satin dress that revealed far more of her considerable cleavage with each heaving breath she took.

"Oh my, your lips are divine, my lord," the lady said, leaning her head back and exposing her long, delicate neck. "Gerald… I can call you Gerald, can't I? And I want you to call me Beth," she purred. "Am I to your liking, Gerald?"

He beheld the curvy blonde, her curls glowing under the soft light of the gas lantern. "Your charms enrapture me," he replied in a low voice. Suddenly, he recalled that his father's best friend, Viscount Bowles, would be in attendance with his family. *Dash it all! Why did I involve myself in this crazy bet tonight of all nights?*

His friends, Victor Thomas and Asher Wright, had bet that he couldn't beat their time in having the lady proposition him.

Gerald was certain he'd won the bet and knew he should return to the ballroom, where his family expected his presence. *Yet I deserve some pleasure,* he reasoned. *Maybe a few more minutes wouldn't hurt. I should be able to claim a little pleasure and make it back to the ballroom before I am missed. I wagered fifty pounds, after all. This will be an easy and pleasurable win.*

She giggled and pressed herself against him, combing her fingers through the back of his hair, as his own hands worked their way toward her ample bosom.

God's teeth! Her gown barely covers those luscious globes.

"Oh, Gerald. We are friends, aren't we?" she said, suddenly beginning to pant.

Why in the world is the woman panting? So far, they'd only kissed. *Blast!* The woman would draw unwanted attention from all the noise she was making.

Clearing his throat, he replied, "Yes…my lady…of course we are."

"Because your friendship is ever so important to me," she said, panting louder. "Isn't it important to you?"

"Why yes, absolutely."

Why is she harping on about friendship? Can she not simply relax and enjoy the moment?

"Oh, I knew you'd agree!" She grabbed him by the ears and yanked him down for an enthusiastic kiss.

He yelped as she dug her sharp nails into his earlobes as though she were hanging on to a runaway horse. "Er…madam, if you will release my ears?" he whispered. Alas, he doubted she could hear him over her vociferous gasping and groaning.

Carefully, he liberated his ears, one at a time. Lady Adamson was a desirable woman, but their interlude was turning out to be the opposite of the heady experience he'd anticipated.

This wasn't as easy as he had hoped. Gerald found himself mentally kicking himself for agreeing to the blasted bet—how long it would take to tempt Lady Adamson to proposition him. Twenty minutes, to be exact. A record. His friends had timed it, of course. They'd stood a few feet behind them in the ballroom at the time. Wright had clocked in at thirty minutes in Hyde Park last week, and twenty-five minutes was all it had taken for Thomas at Almack's three days past.

Even though Gerald had won the bet with his friends, he'd also wanted to claim his pleasure with the voluptuous beauty. The lady's lusty reputation was well-known among the bachelors of the *ton*. She delighted in trysting in the riskiest of settings— often under her elderly husband's nose. Tonight was no different. Lord Adamson had been in the gaming room for the past hour deep in a rematch of piquet against Viscount Simon Wiley.

What Gerald hadn't realized was how exasperating Lady Adamson was. He bit back another yelp as she yanked on his ears again, pulling his face down into her considerable cleavage. She then launched into another energetic round of moaning and panting...

Hell, he'd never hear anyone approaching with the noise she was making.

A chorus of loud gasps sounded behind him.

Too late.

Biting back a curse, Gerald spun around, and the color drained from his face. Standing at the entrance of the gazebo was his father, Lord William Lawrence, the Earl of Bellecote, red-faced with fury, his horrified mother, Lady Mary Ellen Lawrence, the Countess of Bellecote, his father's best friend, Viscount Bowles, and his wife, Lady Fleur Bowles, whose faces were mottled in astonishment. But the most memorable expression was on the face of his betrothed—the Honorable Selena Bowles, daughter of the viscount and his French-born wife.

Gerald couldn't help but notice the poor girl looked less like a debutante and more like a frightened little bird with her mouth agape in shock. Her skinny, petite frame seemed overwhelmed by the poufy pink confection of the gown she wore. Although her dark hair was thick and shiny, the style was far too babyish for his tastes, with fat ringlets framing her pallid, thin oval face. *She looks like a little girl. How in blazes is this child to be my wife?*

The only truly striking quality about the young lady was her eyes. They were quite extraordinary, and Gerald could not recall ever seeing eyes that color. Pale blue—almost translucent—surrounded by a darker blue around the outer rim. Having never seen the like, he felt starstruck, almost being pulled into the depths of those stunning eyes, despite his irritation with the situation.

His father cleared his throat and Gerald jolted, realizing he was staring at the young woman.

"I had hoped for a better reason for your failure to join us when we arrived at the Adamsons' ball." His father nodded at the woman in front of him. "Lady Adamson, your husband is searching the ballroom for you."

A visible shudder shook the woman and her head bobbed in a quick nod.

Gerald was relieved she didn't toss in another moan.

Without a word, Lady Adamson practically leaped from the gazebo, hurrying down the garden path that led back to the ballroom.

"Gerald, I'll see you in my study first thing tomorrow morning," his father growled. "Do not be late."

The next morning

"It was a lark...a dare, Father. Surely you participated in bets in your youth. Or have you never been goaded to do something that you knew wasn't a good idea?" Gerald said in frustration, trying desperately to defend a poor decision—or at least deflect and not create a worse situation. To say his parents were angry and disappointed was an understatement. But if only he could appeal to his father's own experiences after university...

His father roared his response, dashing any hope of Gerald

appealing to his adolescence.

"This is Selena's come-out season, and we were hopeful you would not embarrass us. But you couldn't even give us one night. Instead, you were caught in *flagrante delicto* with Lord Adamson's wife—the hostess of the ball, no less," his father boomed. "Probably one of the most blatantly disrespectful things I've ever known you to do. Had her husband caught you instead of us, it might have been pistols at dawn. The man might be obtuse when it comes to his philandering wife, but he is still known as a crack shot. We might have been planning your funeral, had he called you out."

"Are you saying you've never sown your oats, Father?" Gerald said in his defense.

"Is that what you're calling it these days? In my day—*as today*—cuckolding another man's wife is as low as one can go. No more excuses, son," Lord Bellecote said, his tone low and clipped. It made it hard to win any argument because he was usually so precise and measured, making Gerald or anyone who argued with him sound childish and churlish.

"I've only come down from Cambridge six months ago," Gerald said.

"And you've been acting out ever since," his father shot back.

"And we're back to that again," Gerald snapped. "You've been criticizing me ever since." He took a deep breath and released it slowly. He wasn't a bounder, and when he'd sobered, he'd had enough sense to be embarrassed by his behavior.

He'd been a fool to let his friends dare him to join in the bet. Many of them had already been propositioned by Lady Adamson over the past few months. It had only been a matter of time before she got around to offering up her considerable charms to him.

But somewhere between the drinking and the game room, he'd forgotten it was his betrothed's first Season until he and Lady Adamson were *occupied* in the gazebo. Had he remembered *sooner*, he might have had the wherewithal to take Lady Adamson into the garden shed instead of being led into the gazebo. After all, he'd already won the bet. But instead of claiming a quick kiss and a squeeze and then beating a hasty retreat into the ballroom before he was missed, he'd had to be greedy and indulge himself. Little did he know, Lady Adamson was as cacophonous as she was eager.

"You've crossed a line here, son," his father said finally, his tone now heavy with disappointment.

Gerald felt even more like a heel and wisely kept his mouth shut.

"If you did this to break your betrothal to Selena, you may have accomplished that," his father continued. "This is one youthful indiscretion too many. I'm going to have to do a lot of work to repair what you've done...and so will you. Mark my words."

CHAPTER ONE

Bellwood Estate
Derbyshire, England
Late November 1818

"GOD'S TEETH, APHRODITE!" Gerald ran his hands through her thick sable mane. "You are so much more than I bargained for. You've completely enraptured me. If only you didn't find my ears so worthy of your attention. Our time together would be better spent if you would release your hold on them." He leaned in and whispered, "You're just too impatient, my beauty, because you know I have what you want."

An enthusiastic snort was her reply.

"That's my girl. Here's the reward I promised," Gerald said.

She nickered as he reached into his breeches and pulled out a large, ripe carrot.

Aphrodite munched happily as Gerald reached up and lightly scratched behind her ear.

His newest racehorse had more than earned her treat, having just beaten her fastest practice time. At this rate, she would be ready well before June and Epsom Downs.

He surveyed the refurbished stables with satisfaction. The structure looked nothing like it had when he arrived at Bellwood more than five and a half years ago. Back then, he'd been shocked to see the decay and deterioration of the property.

Grimacing, Gerald recalled being summoned to his father's study the morning after the Adamsons' ball back then. And all because of that blasted bet with Victor Thomas and Asher Wright. The shame he'd felt when his parents discovered him in the arms of the exuberant Lady Adamson—he'd never be able to forget the looks on their faces.

He'd steeled himself for one of his father's long-winded lectures on a gentleman's proper decorum. But there had been no such sermonizing. Instead, it took all of three minutes for his father to strip him of his allowance, amenities, townhouse, and amusements. In three minutes, his father had removed him to a run-down property in Derbyshire. He would have to work to earn his place back in Society and atone for disrespecting their family.

Gerald had been banished without a pound to his name with the understanding that he needed to learn from Angus Connery, the estate manager his father had hired.

"I like the man. If you allow him, he can teach you a great deal, son. If you don't...well, let's not cross that bridge," his father had warned.

Connery came from Scotland with a wealth of knowledge on running a successful estate. In the beginning, Gerald had tried not to like him, but it was impossible. Connery was one of the finest men Gerald had ever known. The Scot had taught him everything from animal husbandry to planting, from harvesting crops to carpentry, to keeping detailed estate accounts.

What had started out as a harsh punishment turned into the best thing that had ever happened to him. After overcoming his initial resentment, Gerald had been determined to prove to his father that he could turn the estate around. Determined to make up for his immature, irresponsible, and reckless behavior. Determined to win back his father's respect.

He was damn proud of his efforts, including his hard-earned calluses. The roof, the interior, and all the horses—everything was new. Gerald loved the stables and had long ago decided this was his favorite place to be. Talking to the horses, while he mucked out their stalls, he would work through problems. The animals seemed to understand he needed someone to listen. When he was ready to tackle the problem, he would then discuss his ideas with Connery.

The renovations on the manor house were near completion. In a week or so, Gerald would be finally ready to welcome his entire family for a visit, and what better time than the Christmas holiday? He couldn't wait to show his home to his parents, his sister Lady Diana Banbury, his esteemed brother-in-law Lord Christopher Banbury, and Gerald's thirteen-year-old sister, Gabby. It had been too long.

The last time he'd seen his family had been last Christmas—almost a year ago. He had gone home to the Bellecote family estate in Sussex. He'd planned to visit his family more often, but there had been so many unexpected problems that cropped up at Bellwood that he hadn't had time to make it back home.

But all of that would change now that the estate was finally functioning smoothly. In the past five years, he'd worked closely under Connery's expert tutelage, turning the failing estate around and making it profitable. What was more, he'd discovered an affinity for estate management.

He'd also discovered a passion for racing horses. With Connery's advice, Gerald had begun to add to his stables. Although he loved to win, he loved to work with the horses even more. The two-thousand-guinea purse he'd won in April with his stallion, Hermes, at Newmarket had given him the additional blunt he'd needed to make necessary repairs to the manor house.

Not only was he winning substantial purses, he had also begun charging handsome stud fees to other peers and landowners seeking to expand their own stables. After discovering a knack for evaluating horseflesh, Gerald was fast gaining a reputation for his expertise.

He'd even noticed a marked change in his physique since moving to Bellwood. He'd always been active, riding every morning and boxing at Gentleman Jackson's, but he'd never done physical labor in his life. Now, he resembled a farmhand more than a viscount—his complexion was tanned from spending so much time outdoors, and his shirts and breeches had become snug given his broadened, muscular frame.

"You would not believe what this place looked like five years ago, Aphrodite," he said as he began to brush her sleek coat. "Father purchased it from Baron Barrows with the intent of renovating it as a wedding gift for when I finally married. The place had been sorely neglected."

Gerald chuckled as Aphrodite offered up a nicker in reply.

Barrows had no talent for management and even less for gambling. He'd nearly bankrupted himself and been forced to sell the estate at auction, which was how Gerald's father had acquired it. The baron's ill treatment of the staff had led to a frequent turnover, which further eroded the property.

But Gerald had discovered a hidden gem in the run-down estate: Baron Barrows had been mad about racehorses. The estate auction had also included several fine thoroughbreds. Eventually, Gerald began to expand the stables. First, he purchased Hermes, a male thoroughbred, then he acquired Aphrodite, and last month, he'd purchased a second filly named Athena. Gerald was counting on their excellent bloodlines to help him win even more races.

"I see ye've been whispering sweet nothings to the lovely Aphrodite. She's already putty in your hands. With the right training, she'll bring you as much good fortune as Hermes has."

Gerald turned to see Connery leaning his shoulder against the stable wall, a grin on his face.

"The horses, they get in your blood, don't they, lad? Not quite like a lass…but close."

"They do indeed." Gerald chuckled. "I've always enjoyed horses. Even caring for other people's horses."

"Aye, I remember when you took care of your sister's horse. I'll never forget the look on her face when we delivered Bandit to your family's estate last Christmas."

"Diana was thrilled," Gerald said, remembering his sister's joyful tears. He'd been so choked up over everything she'd gone through that he'd had to hold back his own emotions.

"Aye, she's a lovely lass, and deserving of a happy life," Connery agreed in his distinctive, deep brogue.

Gerald nodded, thankful for his father's wisdom in hiring Connery. From the first moment they met, the Scotsman had been blunt and honest about the condition of the property and what it would take to fix it. Everything had been in a state of ruin or collapse. The stable's roof had fallen in, and the grounds surrounding the home, including what appeared to have been once beautiful gardens, had been left fallow. The entire place needed restoration.

Connery had been his guide in all things. In fact, the Scotsman had even held the purse strings for the first three years. He approved every purchase, even bags of flour for the kitchen. It was one more way his father had driven his point home. But it didn't matter because Gerald had been determined to make the estate a success and respected Connery's experience and abilities.

"By the way, Wright should be here in a week," Gerald said, finishing his brush-down of Aphrodite. "I invited both him and Thomas to come for the holiday. Wright's family is out of the country, and he's coming. Thomas won't be able to make it, but sends you warm regards for the holidays."

"I look forward to seeing him again," Connery said in an amused tone.

"Yes, my friends have changed." Gerald chuckled again.

"Not as much as you've changed," Connery noted.

"Maybe. But their fathers didn't strip them of their financial resources, send them away, and make them rebuild a derelict estate."

"If I didn't know better, I'd say you've become a positive influence on your friends," Connery countered. "They turn to you for advice about horses and estate management. I've seen the respect they have for you. And Bellwood is no longer derelict. It's one of the most beautiful estates in Derbyshire and is becoming known for its prized horseflesh."

"Thank you for your faith in me," Gerald said, reaching out and shaking his friend's hand.

"You're welcome, my boy. Believe it or not, I've learned a few things from you as well, and it's made me proud. I've managed many estates, but never 'ave I taught someone else. And I believe ye might've surpassed my skills in horse breeding."

"You humble me, Connery," Gerald said. "I hope I will always live up to your faith in me."

"Ach, now dinnae go makin' an old Scot weep," Connery said, "or you'll ruin my reputation for being a cantankerous old bastard."

Gerald threw back his head and laughed, knowing full well that beneath his gruff exterior, Connery had a heart of gold. But he was truly thankful for the older man's advice. Connery had helped him realize what had been missing from his life: purpose. Bellwood and his horses had given him that purpose—and sparked his determination and drive.

Gerald's lips twitched as he realized he would have done the same thing as his father, had he been in the man's shoes. Gerald had been on a path to ruin. Had his family not intervened, who knew what his life would be like today? Over time, Gerald had realized he loved estate management—the responsibilities suited him perfectly. It was something he had never imagined doing, but he'd taken to it like a duck to water.

He was at ease now, having completed much of the work he had set out to do. The manor house, which he intended to rename Bellwood Manor, required a few last-minute touches, which he hoped to accomplish over the next few days.

"And with the holidays and yer family's forthcoming visit, the house is abuzz with excitement," Connery said. "I found the cook and housekeeper in the kitchen with their heads together, drafting a list of duties that took up the entire table. With those two planning things, it portends to be special. Prepare yourself."

He grinned. "I'm looking forward to a merry holiday celebration."

"I'll second that," Gerald replied. He was glad his family was coming to Bellwood instead of his traveling to Sussex. He was looking forward to showing them all the improvements.

According to his mother's recent letter, Selena and her mother would be joining them as well. His mother had written that they wanted to host a small birthday celebration for Selena at Bellwood, given that she would soon turn twenty-one.

Gerald didn't quite know what to think about that bit of news.

Nor did he know what to think about Selena. Although they were essentially strangers, he'd been betrothed to her since he was seven years old.

"We signed a betrothal agreement for you to marry Selena," his father had explained. *"There are things parents do for their children that are for the best. You may not fully understand that now, but eventually you will..."*

But as Gerald came of age, resentment had sparked and grown. He'd pushed the boundaries of his father's patience with his drinking, carousing, gambling, and taking part in outrageous dares with his friends.

The night of the debacle, the family was in London for the Season. The Bowles were there as well for their daughter's come-out. After discovering Gerald with Lady Adamson in a shocking embrace, Lord and Lady Bowles had been as incensed over his flagrant, rakish behavior as his parents and had threatened to break the engagement. Gerald would never forget the wide-eyed astonishment on Selena's fragile features, nor how painfully young and naïve she was.

Somehow, his father had managed to salvage the betrothal. Although Gerald would have preferred to have left it broken, he hadn't fought it at the time, given how angry his father had been. Since then, he had been so preoccupied renovating Bellwood that he hadn't given the girl or the betrothal much thought.

Although he was looking forward to his family's visit, he hoped his parents would not press him about Selena. While the past few years had taught him the importance of duty and hard work, he still had goals to accomplish before he could even contemplate marriage.

Yes, that was it. If his parents brought up the topic, he would simply explain that the timing was not right.

CHAPTER TWO

Rose Point Chateau
Nottingham, England
Two weeks later

SELENA BOWLES HELD her mother's head in her lap, barely resisting the impulse to pull her to her heart and will her to be better. Lady Bowles looked so pale and thin, with damp hair around her face. Only a week ago she was hale and hearty. Selena had never seen her mother so ill, and it had only taken a matter of days.

"*Ma chérie*, you must go…leave while you can," her mother said, her voice reedy and breathy. "Cook will care for me. I cannot protect you—and may not be here much longer. You must go."

"I cannot leave you, *Maman*," Selena whispered, choking on a sob. Taking a clean rag, she dipped it into the bowl of cool water on the bedside table and sponged her mother's fevered brow. Smoothing the strands of dark hair away from her azure eyes, Selena kissed her mother's cheek.

Fighting back tears, she prayed her mother would recover.

We've just lost Papa. I can't lose you too.

Viscount Phillip Bowles had passed away fifteen months ago when his heart finally gave out. He'd been with friends on a hunt;

fortunately, they hadn't traveled far when the attack came on. Acting swiftly, his friends had carried him back to the house as quickly as possible.

His doctor had shaken his head. "There is nothing I can do for him," he had told the viscountess and Selena in private. "I am amazed that he has lived this long—a tribute to his strength of will and generous spirit."

Selena's father had urged them not to fear the future and reassured them about his heir.

"Darlings," her father had rasped on his deathbed, "he is a good and honorable young man. His father, Arthur, and I were cousins and friends when we were young. Percival will take good care of you."

He expressed his love for each of them and, after kissing his wife, took his last breath.

Percival Bowles had been the first officer on board the *Midnight Maiden*, a merchant vessel that had been at sea for nine months until docking in Portugal. It had taken the solicitors an additional six months to locate Percival and inform him of his change in fortune.

Although grief-stricken, Selena and her mother had welcomed the new viscount with warmth and hope in their hearts.

They would realize immediately that Viscount Bowles was anything but honorable.

He was an evil tyrant.

The new viscount went nowhere without his servant, Grom. Percival had swiftly installed the giant brute as the new butler. Poor Higgins, who had served the family for as long as Selena could remember, had been tossed out without a farthing.

"He's lucky to get a reference," Percival had declared.

In fact, Percival and his giant minion had fired all the servants—save for Maggie Ghent, their cook, and her husband Ben, the stable master. It would have been impossible to replace them as quickly as the maids and footmen. Unfortunately, the new servants were as coarse and cruel as their master. Selena realized they were no better than spies who would watch her and her mother like hawks and report everything they did and said to Percival. Selena and her mother took to having their private conversations in the water closet.

And now, just two weeks after Percival's arrival, Selena's mother had fallen ill. The pain was unbearably raw for Selena. Not only had everything changed, but her dear mother was sick.

"You must leave me," her mother repeated hoarsely, snapping Selena from her reverie. "I cannot believe this man to be your father's cousin. His plans for you are evil." Her voice dropped to a whisper. "My darling girl, you must go and save yourself."

"Hush, Maman. The walls have ears." But her mother was right. Only a few days after his arrival, she had patiently explained Selena's betrothal to Viscount Gerald Lawrence. It was expected that they would wed sometime after Selena turned twenty-one.

"And is there something magical about the age of twenty-one?" Percival had sneered.

"My husband and Gerald's father were boyhood friends. Our families have been friends for years," Lady Bowles had repeated. "Selena and Gerald have been betrothed most of their lives. It is hoped their wedding will be forthcoming."

Percival had slammed his fist on the dining table, nearly toppling all the crystal and spilling the wine.

Selena had nearly jumped at his outburst. She'd looked at her mother, who calmly regarded Percival with the regal bearing of a queen. Her father had always said her mother had a spine of steel. Lady Bowles's family had heeded insights and fled to England just before the revolution started in France, establishing themselves in Sussex. Despite their many years in England, their loyalty was occasionally called into focus during the Napoleonic War, elevating the need for her strong spine.

"I'm the new lord here and I will decide Selena's future." Percival had jabbed his fork into a chunk of roast venison and crammed it into his mouth, leering at Selena as he chewed. "Who is this upstart Viscount Gerald Lawrence? I've never heard of him."

"He is the son of the Earl of Bellecote, one of the most esteemed families of the peerage," Lady Bowles had replied in a serene tone. "My husband wrote to your father about the betrothal, and he was happy to hear of it. I am surprised he did not mention it to his son."

Selena had been proud of her mother, who did not flinch under Percival's narrow-eyed glare.

"I will meet with my solicitor and have him notify the Bellecote family that the betrothal is off." He gulped down the rest of his ale, slammed down the empty tankard, and wiped his mouth with the back of his hand. "I shall marry Selena. It would be best for the family, wouldn't you agree, my dear?" He'd turned to Selena with a yellow-toothed smile, revealing several missing bottom teeth. "Unlike my predecessor, my seed is potent and will bear fruit."

Both Selena and her mother had gasped at his crude insult. Selena had felt a frisson of repulsion run through her.

"Wouldn't the late viscount be proud of us?" Percival had continued, spearing another hunk of roast meat. Chewing with his mouth open, he said, "Mmm… This is quite good. I'm glad we kept the cook, Grom." He'd grinned at the burly man who stood beside Percival's chair.

"Yes, your lordship," Grom had replied in a guttural monotone.

Selena blinked back tears, and the back of her neck prickled as she continued to sponge her mother's feverish forehead. Ruminating on that horrible night, she realized her mother had not mentioned the inheritance Selena would gain on her twenty-first birthday. It was the reason for the stipulation in the betrothal that the wedding take place sometime after Selena came of age. Her parents had wanted her to be financially secure in her own right. Both her father and her mother had spoken of it to her. The inheritance had been passed down from her maternal grandmother and included a manor home in Sussex, a townhouse in

London, and her *grand-mère*'s family jewels—which her grandparents had secreted from France with their escape, and which her parents had placed with their solicitor for safekeeping, as well as substantial funds that had been invested when the family relocated to England. Selena had no idea of the total value, but until now had never given it any thought. Her family had frequently used the townhouse when they traveled to London, as well as her mother's family manor house in Sussex, preferring that at times to going home to Nottingham.

Oh, Maman, what are we to do?

Her mother, who had never been sick a day in her life, had started becoming weaker and weaker. Yesterday afternoon, Selena had taken her a cup of tea and discovered that her mother, who'd gone upstairs to take a nap, was limp and her breathing shallow.

Selena had immediately alerted Maggie. But Grom had intercepted the cook on her way out the door to fetch the doctor. He'd ordered her back into the kitchen to prepare the viscount's favorite meal. Maggie had done as much as she could to help Selena's mother, but nothing seemed to be working.

Her mother was dying, and Selena was certain Percival had poisoned her.

"Selena…you must save yourself, my darling," her mother whispered again. "Go to the Earl of Bellecote. Tell him everything. He will keep you safe and do the right thing by you."

A sound at the door made Selena turn in surprise and wipe the tears on her cheeks. Percival and Grom sauntered into the room.

"Please fetch the doctor. My mother is gravely ill and needs assistance," she pleaded.

The two men looked at each other and laughed.

"Get out of my parents' bedchamber. Get out!" she screamed. "You poisoned my mother. I know you did!"

Percival grabbed her by the arms and hauled her up from the chair like a rag doll, smashing her in the face with his meaty fist.

She awoke in confusion, the right side of her face throbbing in pain, and realized she was lying on her bed in her own chamber.

"Cochons!" she exclaimed, then winced at the pain. She'd always resorted to French expletives to express her anger, much to the consternation of her mother and the amusement of her late father.

Somehow, she got up and ran to the door, her knees almost buckling from lightheadedness. How long had it been since she'd seen her mother? She reached for the doorknob and found it was locked. Furious, she pounded on the door. "Let me out! I must see my mother!"

She pounded and screamed until her hands were numb and her voice was hoarse.

Finally, footsteps approached, and a key scratched in the lock.

She stepped back as the door creaked open.

Percival walked in and announced, "Your mother is dead. Tragically, she succumbed to her fever."

Selena gasped, her hands covering her mouth. Fresh tears blurred her vision. "No! It's not true. Please, take me to her now."

"I'm afraid that is not possible. It would be dangerous for you to be near the body. After all, we wouldn't want you to catch what she had. The funeral will be held tomorrow. The cook and her husband are preparing the body for burial.

"Please, I need to see my mother."

He ignored her plea. "Know this. I am your guardian now, and you will obey me." He started to leave but turned around. "Pack a valise and be ready to depart right after your mother's funeral tomorrow. We will be traveling to Gretna Green. For our wedding." He gave her a leering grin as he dragged her against him, holding her arms above her head in a viselike grip against the wall and bruising her mouth in a slobbering kiss.

Foul whisky breath nearly suffocated her, and she barely kept herself from retching. If she was going to get out of this, she needed her wits about her. She could not draw his ire. Not with Grom standing in the doorway, ready to pounce.

"I can't wait for our honeymoon, my dear." Percival laughed, grinding himself against her as he grabbed her breast and squeezed painfully. "And please do your best to fight me in bed. It will be much more enjoyable," he whispered, sinking his teeth into her earlobe.

Selena clenched her jaw at the pain. She was mortified but refused to make a sound. Not from his lecherous assault, and not from his announcement.

He stepped back and looked at her through narrowed eyes. "I see you are learning. It's wise to follow my orders. You will see it's for the best," he said, adjusting his cuffs before leaving the room. A moment later, she heard the key turn in the lock.

She collapsed on her bed and broke into sobs.

Her beautiful, kind-hearted mother was gone. *Maman! What am I going to do without you?* No chance to say goodbye. That devil had murdered her mother as indisputably as if he'd held a gun to her head. Selena was certain of it.

Dizzy and nauseated, she took deep breaths, trying to keep from throwing up.

The last thing her mother had said to Selena was to save herself.

You were right, Maman. It is the only way. She had to leave. Rose Point Chateau was no longer her home. She would follow her mother's advice and travel to London to the home of the Earl of Bellecote, the family of her betrothed.

She would pack, but not for Gretna Green. She would wait until everyone was asleep. Then she would make her escape. Percival had helped himself to her father's fine whisky, guzzling it like water. He'd spent every night since his arrival playing cards with Grom, the two of them drinking themselves into a stupor in her father's library. Surely this night would be no different.

As the house settled for the night, she set her plan in motion. She arranged the pillows on her bed under the covers, to look as if she were sleeping. She blew out the bedside candle and allowed her eyes to adjust to the darkness. Next, she braided her waist-length hair and wrapped it into a coronet around her head. In a basket under the bed, she reached for a canvas sack the maids used to transport soiled linens for washing. Quickly, she reached into a drawer and, without looking, whipped out a few items of clothing, stuffing them into the sack. She had to make this quick.

Opening the drawer of her bedside table, she took out a box of torches. She removed one and set it aside, sliding the box into the bag. She picked up the torch, hefted the sack, and tiptoed to the bookcase at the far end of her bedchamber.

Setting the sack down on the floor, Selena crouched and shifted several books on the bottom shelf. Pressing against the back panel, she moved back as the bookcase sprang open on a well-oiled axis. Picking up the sack, she walked through the narrow opening into a hidden passage. Deftly, she touched another lever and watched as the bookcase slid closed, securing the passageway from prying eyes.

Her parents had shown her the secret passageway when she was a little girl. As a child, she would play hide-and-seek here with her nanny. Sometimes her parents would play with her too. She had so many fond memories of her childhood.

If only she and her mother had had the foresight to make their escape earlier, before it was too late.

She bit her trembling lip as she lit the torch and set it on a small table next to a wooden box. Lifting the lid, she took out a pair of boy's breeches, a shirt, and boots. Removing her gown, she donned the breeches and shirt and put on the boots.

She'd always worn boy's clothes when she went for her morning rides, preferring to ride astride. Her parents had permitted it only on the family estate. She didn't have room in her sack for the gown she wore, so she folded it and left it on a chair next to the table. She reached back into the box and removed a locket, then opened it and gazed at the miniatures within of her beloved mother and father. She kissed both images and snapped the locket closed. Wiping the tears from her eyes, she secured the locket about her neck.

Reaching back into the box, she took out one final item—a small reticule that contained some spending money from her last trip to the village before that devil arrived, and a few jewels her mother and father had given her, including a sapphire ring, her grandmother's pearls, and her father's signet ring, something her mother insisted she have—treasures she'd secured in her secret hiding place shortly after they realized Percival was not the honorable man they'd believed. She wiped fresh tears from her cheeks at the thought of her lovely and wise mother.

Her mother's jewels, along with the household funds for the month, were in a locked safe in her father's library. The first thing the bastard did when he arrived was demand the key to the safe from Selena's mother.

Everything she loved was gone.

I'll just have to make do, Maman.

If she ran out of money, she would have to sell her jewelry.

She tucked her braid into one of her father's floppy hats—one that he always wore in the gardens when he helped her mother prune the roses.

She donned her cloak and looped the sack over her shoulder. Picking up the torch, she carefully made her way through the hidden passage and down a set of stairs that led to the pantry behind the kitchen. In the larder, she found a small wedge of cheese and half a loaf of bread, which she stuffed into the sack. She slipped several apples and carrots into the deep pockets of her hooded cloak before making her way to the stables.

Quiet as a mouse, she saddled the large gray stallion that her father had given her on her eighteenth birthday. The horse nickered upon seeing her.

"Shh! Azure, we must be quiet. We don't want to wake anyone." Taking a carrot, she fed it to her horse. She had named him Azure because in the moonlight his gray coat looked blue, and her father had chuckled that the color matched her own silver-blue eyes. Climbing into the saddle, she whispered to her horse, "We must leave." Without looking back and with tears streaming down her face, she fled in the moonlight.

In one year, she had lost everything—her father, her mother, and all the servants who'd been like family. She wished she could have said goodbye to Maggie and Ben, their cook and stable master, but she couldn't risk being caught by Grom or Percival—or any of his other spies.

She found a small measure of comfort in knowing her parents were together again.

The sky had been overcast when she'd set out just after midnight, and by the time she reached the road that turned toward London, it had begun to rain. Pouring rain.

She muttered a curse. The distance to London was too far in this weather. She looked around in her saddle, searching for some kind of shelter. But nothing was visible. The night was dark, and the rain was cold. London was out of the question.

"Change of plans, Azure," she said in a low voice, surprised when he snorted a reply. She didn't think he could hear her over the downpour. Tugging on the reins, she guided Azure eastward. She recalled that Viscount Gerald Lawrence now resided at Bellwood estate in Derbyshire. She and her mother had planned to join the Bellecote family there for the holidays.

Selena did not know what kind of reception she'd find at Bellwood, given the incident at her come-out all those years ago, but she had no choice. She needed help, and Bellwood was much closer than London.

An hour later, Selena was fighting to keep her eyes awake in the saddle when she heard the rumble of a carriage. Her heart pounding in her chest, she guided Azure off the road, into the woods. Stopping behind a large tree, she waited with bated breath, terrified that Percival had discovered her escape and tracked her down.

"We can't let him find us," she whispered.

As if understanding, her horse stilled, and neither one of them made a sound until long after the dark carriage rolled past.

"I am so glad you're here with me," she whispered, patting her horse's muzzle. "I could not have done this without you."

Azure nickered softly.

Selena heaved a sigh of relief. Taking out her locket, she kissed it and asked her parents for guidance and a bit of luck.

She'd turned to lead Azure back to the main road when she spotted a stream just a few yards away. In her haste, she'd forgotten to fill a pouch of water before she ran away. She said a quick prayer of thanks. She might have been soaking wet from the rain, but her throat was parched.

"We both need water and nourishment, Azure."

Climbing down, she led the stallion to the stream where he could drink his fill. Selena drank as well, feeling much better as she scooped up handful after handful of cool stream water.

Reaching into her pocket, she fed Azure a carrot and an apple. She took a few bites of the cheese and bread and then drank more water.

"At least we have some shelter from the storm," she said.

After she tended to her private needs behind a nearby tree, she walked back to Azure, who greeted her with a snort and a nuzzle on the cheek.

She patted his sleek mane. "All right, we should be on our way, my friend."

She lifted herself onto his back and guided him back onto the road. On the main road, she noticed two wonderful things: the rain had stopped, and the clouds were beginning to dissipate. She pulled out her locket and kissed it again, thanking her parents for guiding her.

As dawn streaked the sky, she happened upon a farmer who gave her directions to get to Derbyshire and the Bellwood estate. Relieved she was heading the right way, she hoped to make it there by nightfall.

When she finally arrived at Lord Lawrence's estate, Selena was completely exhausted and could barely keep her eyes open.

Unfortunately, it had begun to pour again, and she was soaked to the skin, having traveled in the rain for several hours. She turned onto a gently winding path that led to an elegant, white-stoned manor house. Just as she and her horse were almost at the hitching post, a large white dog ran out in front of her, barking, and spooked her exhausted horse. Azure reared up. Unable to keep her seat, Selena tumbled backward, hitting the ground with a thud—and then everything went black.

CHAPTER THREE

Bellwood Manor
Derbyshire, England

GERALD WAS ANTICIPATING a relaxed, leisurely evening. He'd completed a tour of the property's perimeter, looking over the repairs to the numerous breaches in the stone wall that bordered the estate. Satisfied with the results, he'd spent an enjoyable hour playing fetch with Dutch.

The large white dog of uncertain lineage had wandered onto the estate one rainy day two years ago, bleeding and limping. At a loss as to what to do for the animal, Gerald had deferred to Connery, who immediately sent for the doctor.

"Dr. Baker knows how to treat dog wounds?" he'd asked.

"Aye… The man loves dogs. I've seen 'im with them," Connery had replied.

To his surprise, Dr. Baker had known exactly how to set the dog's hind leg. It healed perfectly.

Gerald had named the dog Dutch and begun taking him along as he tended to his duties and chores around the estate. Together, he and Connery had trained the dog to obey key commands. Dutch had proven to be a clever and loyal guardian and protector, especially of the animals. When they'd had trouble with a band of horse thieves last year, Dutch had swiftly cornered one of the bandits in the stables, enabling Gerald and Connery to question the thief to discover the whereabouts of the rest of his gang. Best of all, Dutch was an excellent companion who kept Gerald company on his rambling walks.

Gerald picked up the stick and threw it again, watching the big, lumbering dog chase and return it with the exuberance of a pup. "Good boy, Dutch," he said, crouching to rub the dog's shaggy head. Dutch wagged his tail and hopped about, uttering a mix of woofs, yips, and yaps, his canine chatter making Gerald chuckle.

"Time to head back, boy," he said, feeling the first few drops of rain. As they made their way back to the manor house, the darkening skies abruptly unleashed a fierce storm. Gerald whistled at Dutch, and the two broke into a run as the rain poured down.

By the time Gerald approached the stables, he was drenched to the skin and looking forward to sitting by a warm fire in his study with a snifter of brandy, with Dutch snoozing on his favorite pillow by the hearth.

Dutch had run ahead, and Gerald whistled to call him back. Suddenly, he heard the dog's distinctive bark warning of danger.

Alarmed, Gerald raced around the corner of the stables and stopped in his tracks.

To his horror, a large gray stallion had appeared out of nowhere with a young boy on its back. Gerald shouted another command to Dutch, but to no avail.

The white dog had sprung into attack mode, barking and growling as he lurched toward the horse, causing the stallion to rear up and toss the boy from its back. The horse, kicking and neighing, bolted, leaving the boy on the wet and muddy path.

"Dutch, easy, fella. Easy," Gerald said as he was able to grasp the panting dog's collar and command him to sit. Gerald knelt beside the boy, hoping the youth was all right.

He placed a finger on the boy's neck and felt a strong and steady pulse.

Thank God!

Scooping the boy up in his arms, he got his second shock of the day when the boy's large, floppy hat tumbled to the ground, revealing a long, thick braid.

"My God—it's a girl."

"My lord, I heard barking and shouting," Connery shouted as he ran from the stables.

"I need your help."

"What happened?" Connery asked as he reached Gerald's side.

"Her horse was spooked by Dutch, and the girl fell to the ground," Gerald said. "Help me get her inside."

Connery reached under the girl's head and muttered a curse. He held up his fingers, and Gerald saw they were sticky and dark. "Blood."

"She must have hit her head on a rock when she fell," Gerald said, his fear for the girl increasing.

Shouts from the manor house reached their ears as the front door flew open and his butler and several footmen flew down the steps, carrying lanterns that flooded the area with light.

In the bright glow of the lanterns, Gerald was surprised to see that the figure he held in his arms was no girl, but a young woman.

"I need to get her inside," he said, his voice sounding frantic to his own ears. "Please see to her horse and Dutch."

Connery nodded as Gerald turned and raced up the steps. Behind him, the Scot shouted a stream of orders to the footmen to fetch the doctor, retrieve the runaway horse, and take Dutch inside.

Gerald was greeted by his butler Wells and his housekeeper, Mrs. Evans.

"She has a severe head injury," he said, bolting up the staircase and leaving the capable duo to organize the maids and supplies needed to attend the injured woman. Rushing into the first empty bedchamber off the hallway, he gently laid the young woman on the bed.

Gingerly he probed the back of her head and felt a huge bump. Blood oozed onto his fingers. Muttering a curse, he untied her cloak and eased it from her slender frame. Reaching for the dagger in his boot, he tore a long strip from the bottom of the cloak and tied it snugly around her head, hoping it would stanch the bleeding.

Next, he lightly ran his hands along her legs and arms, carefully checking for breaks and swelling. He sighed with relief. No broken bones.

The young woman moaned and her eyes fluttered open.

He bent over her, and his breath hitched in his throat.

She had the most beautiful blue eyes he'd ever seen.

"L…Lord Lawrence. I f…found you," she whispered.

Complete and utter shock gripped him.

Could it be?

Her face creased in pain, and her eyelids fell closed as a moan escaped her.

Those eyes…

He'd only ever seen such striking eyes once before.

At the Adamsons' ball.

Pale blue, almost translucent, with a dark blue outer rim.

My God, it must be her!

Selena Bowles.

But how? And why was she here? And where was her mother, Lady Bowles?

As if in response, Selena muttered her mother's name, and a tear squeezed past her closed eyelid, trailing down her face.

Gently, he wiped it away with his thumb, leaving a streak across her mud-caked cheek.

He raked his hands through his hair, having trouble making sense of this.

He was taken aback. More than taken aback. He was dumbfounded.

He blew out a ragged breath.

She's not supposed to be here. She was meant to arrive in a few weeks with her mother and his parents for Christmas. *So we can become better acquainted.*

Hell, they weren't acquainted at all.

Gerald had already decided to speak with his parents about putting off the wedding. At first, he'd told himself it was because he still had much to accomplish at Bellwood.

But the truth was that he didn't want an arranged marriage.

He wanted what his parents had, a loving union that had stood the test of time. He wanted what his sister Diana had with the Marquess of Banbury, a partnership of equals—full of love, laughter, and passion.

"Oh God, oh God, oh God!" A terrible thought flashed in his mind. Diana had been thrown from her horse a few years back and the accident had left her blind. Thank goodness her sight eventually returned. But it wasn't immediate—nor had it been expected.

He prayed Dr. Baker would get there soon.

The young woman moaned again, muttering something unintelligible.

He laid his hand over hers, giving her fingers a gentle squeeze. "Everything's going to be all right. I promise." Guilt washed over him. He may have decided he couldn't marry her, but he certainly didn't want her to be in pain or suffer.

All these thoughts swirled through his mind in a matter of moments as he watched over her. If he hadn't seen her eyes, he would never have guessed it was Selena. Her face was caked with mud, and the makeshift bandage he'd wrapped around her covered her entire forehead. Her braid had come unraveled, and her long, dark hair lay in tangles over her shoulders. Slowly, he reached out to move the wet hair from her face, but jumped back like a guilty boy caught with his hand in the biscuit tin as a flurry of footsteps approached.

"My lord, we are here, do not fear," Mrs. Evans said as she bustled into the room, followed by three maids with armfuls of supplies. The older woman clucked her tongue like a mother hen as she took in the small, wan figure on the bed. "Poor wee lass."

"I wrapped a cloth around her head injury. She has no broken bones," he explained as the maids arranged the various items next to the bed, including a large pot of steaming water, soap, bandages, washcloths, and clean towels.

Gerald's eyes watered as one of the maids poured vinegar into the steaming water. He trusted Mrs. Evans, who had a true gift when it came to tending wounds and various ailments.

"Rest assured, my lord, the lass is in good hands," she said, patting him on the arm. "I instructed the lads to ready a hot bath for you. And the cook prepared a hearty beef stew for supper." She waved him off. "Off you go, now. I'm sure you have plenty to discuss with Angus."

Hands on her hips, she gave him a firm nod, effectively dismissing him.

Gerald sighed, trusting that Selena was in good hands. He slipped out, closing the door behind him.

Mrs. Evans was right. She would see to Selena's care until Dr. Baker arrived.

His mind was bursting with questions, and the only way he could get any answers was to speak to the young woman who was currently lying in a bed in his guest room, unconscious with a head injury.

CHAPTER FOUR

HER EYES OPENED to a beautiful blue sky. No, not a real sky, but a breathtaking mural. Like gazing up at the heavens. Rays of sunlight peeked from behind fluffy white clouds that seemed to be chasing each other. The mural extended down the wall to just above the bed's headboard with a glorious scene depicting a three-storied, pastoral manor bordered by delicate lavender wisteria and roses in various shades of pink. She was especially drawn to the image of a majestic oak tree on the emerald-green grounds, a whimsical child's swing hanging from a sturdy branch.

She smiled and breathed out a deep sigh.

What a lovely painting.

She shifted in the bed and gasped at the sudden, sharp throbbing at the back of her head. Tentatively, she touched the raised bump covered in a thick bandage.

"Where am I?" she whispered, choking on a gasp as another sharp pain twisted her ribcage. "Oh, goodness, that hurts!" she cried out. With every movement, a new, agonizing ache made itself known. A slight snore from somewhere to her right seized her attention, and she sat up and promptly plunked back down as the world started to spin. Closing her eyes, she breathed deeply, trying to minimize the misery radiating from every muscle.

"Selena, you're awake," a deep, sleep-roughened male voice said, coming from the same direction of the snore. "Selena, are you all right? Can you speak?"

Her eyelids fluttered open, and she regarded the man connected to the voice. He hovered over her, his face a study in concern.

"Selena?" she croaked and cleared her throat. "Please. Water?"

Swiftly the man filled a cup with water from a pitcher on the bedside table and, carefully sliding his arm under her shoulders, eased her up so she could sip.

She drained the glass and nodded her thanks. "Who is S-Selena?"

"You're Selena," he said.

"I am Selena?" She stared at him, although she had no idea what she wanted to see. He appeared kind and gazed directly at her. *Why can't I remember my name?* She only had his word for it, but he seemed honest enough. She should be upset. She should be crying. But oddly, she found herself quite calm at this revelation. Perhaps because the pain radiating throughout her body left little room to feel anything else.

"You don't remember who you are?"

Slowly, she shook her head.

His face creased with concern, which was a pity because he had a very nice face. More than very nice. He was extremely handsome—so tall and with such broad shoulders. His dark hair, like sable, curled around his collar. How endearing. As though he'd forgotten to have it trimmed. But it was his eyes, warm and brown like fine brandy, that captivated her. She had a ridiculous urge to stare into his eyes for hours.

"You arrived last evening in the middle of a freezing rain-storm," he continued. "Your horse became spooked by my dog and threw you. Your head hit a rock when you fell."

She reached up and felt the egg-shaped bump again. She could feel a raised ridge on top of the bump that felt like stitches. "That explains why everything hurts from my head to my toes."

"I can imagine." He smiled.

Lord, his smile makes him even more handsome. How is that even possible?

"Do you recall anything that happened last night?"

She closed her eyes and tried as hard as she could to remember. But her mind was a complete blank. "I don't—" Her reply was interrupted by a very loud growl coming from the vicinity of her stomach. Her cheeks heated with a blush. "Forgive me. My mind may have forgotten everything, but my stomach clearly remembers."

He chuckled. "Do you feel like you could keep food down?

"I could try."

"Good, because my cook, Mrs. McDonald, is anxious to make you anything and everything you'd like." He reached for the bellpull and tugged.

A soft knock sounded on the door a few moments later.

"Enter."

A petite young maid stepped into the room and bobbed a curtsey. "Yes, my lord?"

"Good morning, Anna," Lord Brown Eyes said. "Can you ask Mrs. McDonald to prepare a tray with a light breakfast?"

"Yes, my lord." The smiling maid gave another quick curtsey and left.

Lord Brown Eyes pulled the chair closer to Selena's bedside and sat. "You arrived last evening during a terrible rainstorm, astride a gray stallion," he said. "At first, I thought you were a boy, given that you were wearing boys' clothes along with a big hat that covered most of your face. I realized my mistake when your cap fell off and your hair unfurled."

Confusion, frustration, and a whole host of other emotions swirled through her at his explanation. "Is the horse all right?

How is your dog?" She hated the thought that either animal may have been hurt in the storm.

Lord Brown Eyes nodded. "Yes, they are both fine. Azure, your stallion, is a magnificent animal."

"How do you know his name?" Her father must have named it, which made her wonder why he named it after a color.

"His name is engraved in the saddle, along with a message from your father, wishing you a happy birthday."

Her father had gifted her with a stallion for her birthday? She had so many questions. "I see. Well, it seems you have me at a disadvantage, my lord. You called me Selena. What is my full name?"

"Lady Selena Bowles."

"Selena Bowles." Nothing. No recognition of her name. She swallowed as panic began to overtake every other emotion churning in her gut.

"Your father was Viscount Phillip Bowles, and your mother is Countess Fleur Bowles." He withdrew something from his waistcoat pocket. "Perhaps this will help." He handed her a gold filagree locket on a long chain. "Mrs. Evans, the housekeeper, found this around your neck when she and the maids were attending you last night."

She opened the locket and gazed at the image of a handsome man with dark hair and gray eyes on one side and a beautiful woman with dark hair and blue eyes on the other. She swallowed the lump in her throat as she touched both miniatures with a trembling finger.

A sudden thought flashed in her mind. "You said *was*," she rasped. "About my father. You said he *was* Viscount Bowles."

"Yes." Lord Brown Eyes blew out a deep breath. "Your father passed away more than a year ago."

Tears sprang to her eyes, and she turned away from him and wiped them away. *My father is gone.* "Where is my mother?"

"I assume she must be at your family's estate in Nottingham. I believe it's called Rose Point Chateau. Does the name of your home spark any recognition?"

Saying the name out loud sent a strange jolt to her heart. As if something bad may have happened. But her memories were foggy, and despite her best efforts, there seemed nothing for her to grasp. She shook her head. "No."

"Your father's solicitors searched for his heir for many months. I haven't heard if they found him."

Pain stabbed her heart at his revelation. "An heir? That means I have no brother..."

"That is true, Selena."

Her father's solicitors were required to search for his heir. Unease pricked the back of her mind, but she couldn't fathom why. Searching her memory, she stared down at the locket still open in her hand. She looked up and found him staring at her, a strange expression in his dark eyes. "M-my apologies. I do not who you are. Nor how we know each other."

He seemed to hesitate as he combed his fingers through his hair. "I am Viscount Gerald Lawrence," he replied. "Our parents are friends."

"I see," she said. "You mentioned my father's estate is in Nottingham? What of your estate?"

"Bellwood is in Derbyshire, although this is an estate my father purchased for me to rehabilitate. Our family estate is in Sussex."

"I must have traveled almost two days to get here..." Her eyes widened and she clapped a hand over her mouth. "How do I know that?"

He reached for her hand again and held it between his. His hands felt warm and comforting.

"Perhaps it's a sign that your memory is returning?"

"Yes, that seems like it would be a good sign." She found it hard to form a thought, but it had nothing to do with her lack of memory and everything to do with his big, warm hands holding hers. "But why did I come here? Alone and in a terrible rainstorm?" She realized she'd uttered those questions aloud. "There had to be a reason, but what was it?" A memory tickled from behind the weeds of confusion. Yet no matter how hard she tried, she couldn't move past those weeds. "Why can't I remember?" Her voice trembled.

"You were left unconscious from your fall. All night, in fact. The doctor who examined you and treated your injuries will return this morning. I am certain Dr. Baker will be able to enlighten us. But I suspect your memory loss may be connected to your head injury."

She shook her head. "I feel as though I am walking through a thick fog. Completely lost."

"I understand how frightening and confusing this must be for you, Selena, but please understand you are safe here. I've already sent word to my parents in London. Together we'll do everything we can to help you. I'm certain Father will send a missive to alert your mother as to your whereabouts."

"Th-thank you, my lord."

"Please call me Gerald," he said.

She gave him a wobbly smile. "Gerald." Although she enjoyed thinking of him as Lord Brown Eyes. Somehow, it seemed more familiar.

"Good." He smiled back.

"So, I am Selena Bowles." Knowing her name gave her the strangest feeling. It was as if she stood outside a window watching someone else live her life.

Gerald gave a slow nod.

There was something that she wanted so badly to remember, but no matter how hard she tried, it was just out of reach. She lifted the locket once more and gazed at the miniatures of her mother and father, hoping, praying for a glimmer of memory. Something…anything. "I feel such sorrow."

"Perhaps learning about your father has brought on this sadness along with your memory loss and your injuries."

"I suppose…but it feels like it just happened…this terrible loss."

"Selena, try to relax and let your memories surface on their own. I feel certain you *will* remember. For now, let us focus on getting you stronger," Gerald said.

She wanted to see Azure. "Can I see him? My horse?"

"Yes. When the doctor permits you, I shall take you to the stables."

She blinked back a fresh wave of tears. Although the viscount was a stranger, he was kind, gentle, and genuinely concerned for her welfare. There had to be a reason why she'd ridden on horseback in a rainstorm to come here, to Bellwood. To him. If only she could remember why. There were no answers—only a growing list of questions. She was a stranger to herself. Until her memory returned, everything about her life would remain a mystery…

Rose Point Chateau
Nottingham, England

"GROM!" PERCIVAL BELLOWED. *Where is that giant idiot?* He wanted his breakfast. He was starving. The day before, they'd buried Lady Bowles in a small cemetery behind the manor. The morning was wet and very cold, and he'd unfortunately slept in longer than he should have. They'd spent the evening playing cards and drinking. He'd fallen asleep with his head pillowed on the generous bosom of one of the maids that Grom had hired.

Grom had done well, hiring several former tavern wenches for the manor. Aye, they certainly knew their business. Percival chuckled as he rubbed his hands together. Although he would soon be married to that little chit locked upstairs in her room, it didn't mean he had to put an end to his various enjoyments.

Nevertheless, they were running late. He and Grom had ridden half a mile from the manor house to the isolated family graveyard, only to discover the gates were locked. Percival remembered he had fired the groundskeeper, who'd left without turning over his keys. Luckily, Grom was adept at picking locks and made short work of the gate.

The graveyard, cold and desolate, had made Percival's skin crawl. It was surrounded by a dark iron gate and was about half a mile behind the stables. A large oak tree stood like a sentry on the outside of the front fence. A flat wagon driven by two footmen rambled down a ruddy road in the spitting rain, carrying the wooden casket bearing Lady Bowles. The reverend walked behind it.

They hadn't bothered waking the dead woman's daughter. He didn't need a weeping girl on his hands.

"I'm here, Vern." The hulking man strode into the study carrying a large tray. He set it down on a table by the window.

"Don't call me that. I am Lord Percival Bowles. Don't ever forget it. We can't let anyone find out, or both you and me will end up swinging by the gibbet."

He had known the real Percival Bowles—they had been friends, or Bowles thought they were. Vern had one friend—himself. That made it easy. After Bowles had told him about the solicitor's letter telling him he was now an earl, Vern decided this was his opportunity. When Bowles came in a little drunk for their celebration, he hit him from behind. *That's one body that will never be found,* he thought.

"Yes, your lordship," Grom said in his deep, flat voice.

"I'm starving. What took so long?"

"The kitchen maid said the cook ran out of rashers and prepared a stew instead."

"We'll be setting off after I eat. Where is the girl?"

"The maid said she's still sleeping. She felt sorry for the girl and let her sleep late because her mother died," the butler said.

"Hmm, remind those maids their loyalty is to me, not that little chit."

"Yes, my lord."

"And make sure you find that groundskeeper and retrieve

those keys. There's no telling what other things he took."

"Yes, my lord."

Vern grinned. "And let me know when the girl wakes. May-hap I'll go up and help her dress for the journey." He threw back his head and laughed.

"I will…your lordship," Grom said as he turned to leave.

Vern dug into the hearty stew. The cook had outdone herself. He'd never eaten so well in his life. It was a pity he wouldn't be able to enjoy the fine fare much longer. He had big plans, and that fine young lady upstairs was the key to making all his dreams come true. He raised his tankard of ale in a silent salute and gulped it down.

As Vern finished eating, a great yawn came over him. Damn, he was still tired. Well, a short nap wouldn't do any harm. He went to the comfortable settee and was practically asleep when his head hit the pillow.

A clap of thunder awakened him with a start. The sky outside the window was dark and gloomy. "What the blazes?"

"My lord… My lord… Vern! Vern, wake up!"

Vern felt as though he were swimming up from the dark depths of a murky lake. He realized someone was shaking his shoulders and shouting in his ear.

"Vern! Wake up!"

He cracked his eyes open and looked up at the giant hovering over him.

"What in the blazes? I told ya never to call me Vern, you lummox!"

"Well, when I called you 'my lord' you weren't waking, so I thought I'd try Vern."

"Help me up, you oaf."

"You fell asleep, my lord."

"Yes, I know. What time is it?"

"It's after three."

"Three in the afternoon?"

"Yes, my lord."

"Why the hell didn't you wake me sooner?"

"Because I was asleep too."

"Why the hell were you asleep?

"Because I was tired."

"Where's the girl?"

"I haven't seen her," Grom returned.

"Dammit! Go and wake her. Have one of the maids go with you. She needs to get up and get dressed. We have to leave for Gretna Green. It will be dark soon, and now we'll have to travel all night."

A few minutes later, Grom rushed back into the room. "She's gone!"

"What do you mean, she's gone? When? She was asleep," Vern said. "How did that happen?"

"I think we were drugged, my lord," Grom said. "I think everyone was drugged."

"What the hell are you talking about?" Vern demanded.

"The stable master and the cook. They're gone too. I think it was that stew. We all ate some, you, me, the footmen, and the maids. We all fell asleep. I only just woke up a few minutes before I came to wake you."

"I want the entire estate searched, including the surrounding properties and all the tenant cottages," Vern demanded. "Find them and bring them to me."

"Yes, my lord," Grom said as he turned and left.

Vern Stiles cursed. *No one makes a fool of me! When Grom finds that bitch, I'll teach her a lesson she'll never forget.*

CHAPTER FIVE

The next morning
Bellwood Estate
Derbyshire, England

GERALD AWOKE WITH a start. Disoriented, he wondered what he had caused him to awaken.

A soft groan came from the bed.

Selena!

He sprang up from his chair and went to her side.

Her head moved restlessly on the pillow. Another whimper escaped her. "Maman, I did as you bid. The fiend won't find me..."

Confused and concerned at her words, Gerald swiftly lit the candle on the bedside table and felt her forehead. Her skin felt hot and dry. Her cheeks were flushed. But her teeth were chattering.

"Azure, we must get to Bellwood before the fiend finds out and comes after us... Maman, where are you?" Emitting another cry, Selena thrashed from side to side. "I'm safe, but where are you, Maman?"

"Good God!" Alarmed, Gerald yanked the bellpull by the bed to alert the servants.

Was she having a nightmare or reliving a horror she'd gone through?

"Selena, it's Gerald. Can you hear me?"

She continued to moan and move restlessly, her eyes still closed.

He reached for a cloth and dampened it with water from the pitcher on the bedside table. Sitting on the edge of the bed, he began to gently bathe her face and neck.

He couldn't understand it. Despite her lack of memory, Selena seemed to be doing well. When Dr. Baker had examined her yesterday morning, he'd affirmed that she did indeed have amnesia, resulting from her fall, but he was optimistic that as she healed, her memory would return.

Gerald had regretted rushing out of her room yesterday morning after Anna arrived with the breakfast tray. He'd hastily washed and dressed and then tackled a few chores, trying to get his mind off...*her*.

Selena had taken hold of his thoughts since her impromptu arrival. The night of the rainstorm she'd been soaked and covered in dirt and mud from her fall. Gerald could barely tell what she looked like. After he'd brought her to the guest room and then left her in the capable hands of Mrs. Evans and the maids, he'd returned after Dr. Baker concluded his examination.

Walking into the room, he'd beheld a vision that left him breathless.

No longer the plain, tiny little bird he'd briefly encountered six years ago the night of the Adamsons' ball, Selena had grown into a stunningly beautiful woman. Long, silky, dark hair framed a lovely face with alabaster skin, a lush, full mouth, and those eyes... Those incredible, translucent blue eyes.

And when she woke up that morning, she was full of questions. It was all he could do to form coherent sentences as she'd peppered him with queries about what had brought her to his home. He'd wanted to tell her about their betrothal but held back. He'd already told her a lot, and it had been most distressing for her. He didn't want to add to that.

Yes, that was the excuse he'd given himself.

But deep down, he just couldn't bring himself to reveal everything. Not yet.

Because if he told her they were betrothed, he would have to tell her the truth…

Uh, yes, well, our first meeting was quite memorable. You and your parents and my parents had just discovered me in a sordid kiss with Lady Adamson in her gazebo, the night of the ball she'd hosted with her much older husband, Lord Adamson. You see, that unseemly kiss was just part of a bet between my idiot best friends and myself. Oh, and by the by, I won the bet.

Of course, my father figuratively tore a strip off my back the next morning and basically banished me to Bellwood as my punishment, while he apologized to your parents and attempted to salvage our betrothal. He succeeded in that, but with the stipulation that we were not to marry until after you came of age and came into an inheritance from your maternal grandmother. Your parents wanted you to be independent should things go awry again. And here I am still at Bellwood, five years later, a little wiser, hopefully. The rest, as they say, is history…

Had he admitted the truth to her, she would have no doubt been shocked. Hell, she might have broken the betrothal that his father had worked so hard to save.

Wasn't that what he wanted, though? A broken betrothal?

But everything is different now.

Isn't it?

A quick knock sounded on the door to the chamber before it opened, admitting Anna. "My lord, is anything amiss?" Her face showed concern. Understandable, since it wasn't even dawn yet.

"Miss Bowles has developed a high fever. Please inform Mrs. Evans and send for the doctor as soon as possible."

"Right away, my lord," Anna said with a quick nod before rushing out of the room.

Gerald was dipping the cloth in the water again when Selena made another sound of discomfort.

"Alone… Not safe…"

"You *are* safe," Gerald whispered. "And you are not alone. I promise." Gently he wiped her fevered brow, his worry escalating with each passing minute.

He couldn't understand it. Where had this fever come from? She'd been alert last evening, her cheeks tinted with a pinkish hue. He'd assumed it was because she was on the mend. Little did he know that the color infusing her cheeks may have been the beginning of her fever.

Dr. Baker had given Gerald a positive prognosis after examining Selena yesterday morning.

"Miss Bowles is a strong young woman," the physician had said. "I am hopeful she will make a full recovery."

Gerald had been relieved. He'd ventured back into Selena's room with Dr. Baker's advice to share as much as he could with her about her life and answer any questions she might have. The one topic he avoided was their betrothal. He had too much guilt twisting through him at how he'd treated her and their engagement.

"It will help in her recovery," Dr. Baker had said before he left.

Indeed, Gerald and Selena had stayed up late last evening talking. She'd asked dozens of questions, and he'd found himself sharing details about his life that he hadn't shared with anyone, outside of his own family.

It was a strange situation, yet he'd felt at ease with her. Talking with her and telling her about his family and his life at Bellwood had been truly enjoyable.

Selena was an intelligent and engaging young woman with a clever sense of humor.

He'd told her about his own life and revealed the little he knew about hers—much to his disgrace. His father and hers had been friends since boyhood. He recalled his shame when he realized she was much more curious about him and his family.

Gerald had told her as much as he dared.

The evening had been pleasant and gone by so fast that he didn't recall when he'd nodded off in the chair.

And now she's burning with fever and trapped in a nightmare. God knows if she'll survive.

Gerald raked his hands through his hair in agitation when another groan brought his attention back to Selena.

"He locked me in my room… That demon. Percival…"

Tears flowed from her closed eyes, wrenching Gerald's heart.

"Selena, you're having a bad dream. I'm here," he said, taking her hand in his.

She whimpered. "…so dirty. He kissed me. Couldn't breathe. Said vile things… Maman, I'm so sorry," she cried.

Dear God, what have you been through? And who's Percival?

The gut-wrenching pain coursing through him was only surpassed by the burning anger he felt at what Selena had suffered at the hands of this bastard named Percival.

And then Gerald recalled his mother's letter. She'd informed him that the late viscount's solicitors had taken months to track down the heir—a cousin by the name of Percival Bowles. He'd been a first officer aboard a merchant ship. The man was clearly a brute.

Gerald reached out and caressed her cheek—it was burning with fever.

"Selena, you're safe, my darling. I'm here. I'll protect you. I promise." He wished his parents were there. They might know what had led to this horrific situation. "Selena…please, open your eyes," he rasped, caressing her cheek. "You are safe. Everything will be fine, I promise."

Her eyelids fluttered open, and she looked at him, her translucent eyes burning with fever. "It's y-you," she whispered. "Y-you're here. You were there… in the storm. S-so kind…so noble. You helped me… I'm so l-lucky. So lucky to have you…"

Gerald swallowed at the revelation, fever or no fever. Was she referring to her status as his betrothed? This young woman had ridden in a rainstorm to the point of exhaustion and fallen at his feet from her horse. He would have been a complete cad if he hadn't helped her. "Many people would have helped you."

"But I needed you," she said in a broken voice. "I came here for a reason—even if I d-don't know why…"

He wished he knew why, too. He surmised it had to do with that bastard Percival, but he needed to know everything. *My God, he was desperate to know what Selena had gone through. And when he did, he would deal with Percival Bowles.* But at present, he had far more pressing worries than her lack of memory—with this raging fever, he feared for her very life.

He bent closer to bathe her forehead and was taken aback by her sudden movement as she grasped his shirt and tugged him down to kiss him.

Gerald's mind swirled as she pressed her lips against his. They were soft and vulnerable and heated from her feverish state. Her guileless, fumbling kiss and the soft moan that escaped her were his undoing. Her innocently innate passion and the look in those beautiful blue eyes mesmerized him, and he abandoned his good sense. Uttering a helpless groan, he pulled her up against his chest, wrapping his arms around her, and deepened the kiss.

He was lost, lost in the pure bliss of kissing Selena. He moved his hands up and down her slender back. Her nightgown was damp and plastered to her body like a second skin. She felt like heaven. He could not believe he'd ever thought her skinny. Her petite frame was deliciously formed with curves that fit his hands perfectly. Her breasts, pressing against his chest, made him feel as feverish as she was.

"I love you, Gerald," she said in a breathy voice, and it was like a bucket of cold water splashed in his face.

What am I doing? She's a complete innocent, he reminded himself. *And I'm acting like a complete cad!* Selena was injured. Worse…he knew she didn't know what she was doing. Hell, she couldn't even remember who she was. Not to mention, Mrs. Evans would be rushing into the room at any moment.

"I'm so sorry, love." He pulled back and gently set her back down against the pillows.

"More kissing," she whispered, a half-smile on her lovely lips, her eyes closed as though she were dreaming. "Love your k-kisses. Love you…"

Oh God! She didn't even know what she was saying. Gerald couldn't help but smile at her impishness. The girl was delirious, and here she was flirting with him, making declarations of love.

"I love kissing you too. But it will have to wait. You need to get better." He kissed his index finger and touched her lips just as a knock sounded on the door.

Blowing out a breath, he tucked the blankets around Selena's shoulders and stood to open the door.

"My lord, my apologies—I was in the kitchen helping Cook when Anna found us and told us everything," Mrs. Evans said as she bustled into the room with the young maid. "Rest assured, I sent young Joshua to fetch the doctor. That boy is faster than a fox on a hunt. Cook and I prepared a mustard poultice and willow bark tea to help bring down the fever."

"Good. Very Good." Gerald rubbed the back of his neck, stepping out of the way as Anna set a tray next to the bed.

"Cook has a hearty breakfast ready for you, and some good, strong coffee," Mrs. Evans told him.

"My thanks, Mrs. Evans." He glanced at Selena, reluctant to leave.

"My lord." The housekeeper reached out and touched his hand. "We must see to Miss Bowles's comfort. We'll let you know when the doctor arrives."

Gerald felt a flush creep up his neck. Had Mrs. Evans guessed something?

He gave a hasty nod and left. Striding to his room, he felt a flurry of emotions churning through him. That kiss. Those lips. Those eyes. But he was all too aware of how vulnerable Selena was. How innocent. What made her leave her home and travel in a rainstorm on horseback to Bellwood? To him. His mind was full of questions and the haunting words that Selena had uttered in her delirium.

He had to find out the truth. He had to keep her safe.

CHAPTER SIX

AFTER HE WASHED and changed, Gerald made his way to the stables. He needed to work. To keep busy. Or he would go mad. He couldn't understand how Selena could take such a turn for the worse. Last evening, she'd seemed better, stronger. And now, she was burning with fever. And top of it all, he'd taken advantage of her. He hadn't meant to, but he'd been so surprised by her unexpected kiss—her unexpected adulation, her sweet sensuality—that he couldn't help himself.

Selena was no longer the young girl who'd reminded him of a frightened bird. Rather, she had grown into a swan—undoubtedly the most beautiful young woman he had seen in many years. And those eyes, those incredible eyes captivated him—drew him to her like a moth to a flame.

And her voice—that sensual, husky voice… The kind of voice that would drive any man wild, the kind he would love to hear whisper "good morning" in his ear.

He ran his hands through his hair in agitation. *Good God! I'm an animal. The poor girl went through a harrowing experience and cannot even recall her own name, and here I am thinking about her whispering in my ear in bed!*

And yet she had revealed her feelings for him. He wasn't used to a woman causing him to blush. She seemed…fond of him. How could that have happened? He had spent very little time with her—and their time together at her come-out, all those years ago, had been a disaster.

Shame shot through him as he recalled that night. That silly bet. The memory of being caught with the cloying Lady Adamson brought a shudder. His behavior certainly couldn't have elevated Selena's trust in him. When she arrived, she had called him Lord Lawrence. Certainly, she would remember that night, too, if she regained her memory.

Gerald had worked hard for over five years to change himself and transform this estate. Suddenly, the thought of Selena possibly losing her regard for him made his chest twist with hurt.

He was so lost in his thoughts, he narrowly avoided knocking down a footman carrying a tray of food.

"My lord, I was just bringing a tray of bacon-and-egg sandwiches to you," the footman said. "Mrs. McDonald said you hadn't broken your fast yet, and thought you and Mr. Connery might enjoy these."

"Thank you," Gerald said, grabbing a sandwich and taking a bite. Mrs. McDonald was not only an excellent cook, she was also a jewel. He took another bite of the delicious sandwich, not realizing how hungry he had been.

"And Wells said to tell you the doctor has arrived and is with Miss Bowles."

"Very good. I'm relieved to hear that," Gerald said. "Ask Wells to have the doctor meet me in my study before he leaves."

"Yes, my lord," the footman said, bobbing his head. "I'll see it done."

"I'll take those for Mr. Connery," Gerald said, grabbing the rest of the wrapped sandwiches from the tray.

Walking into the stables a few minutes later, he noticed Connery was brushing the coat of Azure in the stall. "I'm glad to find you here." Gerald handed the man the wrapped sandwiches. He had already devoured two on his way to the stables.

"How is the girl?" Connery asked.

"Not well. She awoke this morning burning with fever. Baker

is with her now." Gerald rubbed his brow and then reached out to pat Azure. "She doesn't remember who she is. Even though she acknowledged me by name when she arrived."

"Let her spend time with her stallion when she gets past the fever," Connery suggested. "It can't hurt. And it might spark her memory."

"You make a good point," Gerald said.

"This stallion is clearly descended from a strong lineage. Does she remember that her father gifted her the horse?"

"Unfortunately, no," Gerald said with a shake of his head. "It's odd. She murmured things this morning in her fevered state—things that were either a nightmare or a horrible experience that she was running away from."

"Whatever made her come here, she is safe, and we'll do everything we can to help her," Connery said.

"Yes, we will…"

Connery regarded Gerald thoughtfully as he finished eating. "But I sense there's something else that troubles you, lad."

Gerald shook his head. "It's nothing. I am concerned about Miss Bowles, is all." How could he possibly tell Connery that he'd kissed Selena—had taken advantage of her delirious state?

"Pardon, my lord, shall I saddle Aphrodite?" Joshua, the stable boy, said as he set down the basket of apples he'd been hefting.

"Nay, not at the moment. I'll return later to take her out."

"Yes, my lord." The boy nodded.

Connery tossed a sandwich to Joshua, giving him a wink.

"Thank you, sir," the boy said, grinning as he turned to complete his other chores.

Azure gave a soft snort and shook his mane. Gerald reached out and patted the horse, who seemed clearly agitated.

"Azure has the most unique eyes I've ever seen on a horse. He is well named," Connery said.

"They look like Selena's eyes," Gerald blurted. "Where could her father have found such a horse?"

"I don't know, but I'm going to check around. I have a feeling

Azure is descended from a strong line. Might be worth having." Connery chuckled. "Well, that is…might be worth having another one around. I keep forgetting she's your betrothed."

"She's nothing like I remember. She's…"

"Beautiful," Connery finished.

"Yes, she is," Gerald said as he fed Azure an apple.

"Aye, and no matter what she's been through, she's a resilient lass."

"Yes, she is that too."

The sound of a throat clearing drew their attention. Gerald turned and saw the doctor approaching, a grave expression on his face. "Dr. Baker, I was going to head to my study to await you."

"Your footman told me you were out here, and I wanted to tell you as soon as I could." The older man took a deep breath. "I must apologize, Lord Lawrence. It seems that when I initially cleaned Miss Bowles's head wound, I thought I had removed all the dirt and debris. But her fever indicates an infection has set in. I reopened the wound and found a small bit of gravel that I had missed." He shook his head. "I think it may have caused the problem. I am so sorry that I missed it."

Gerald listened and then nodded. "Her hair was matted with rain and mud that night. And there was so much blood, I can imagine that made it more difficult to treat the wound."

"But I do have hopeful news. Her fever has already begun to come down. She is a strong young lady, and although it will take time, I have every reason to believe she will recover. She will require a great deal of care and attention in the meantime."

"She won't lack for that," Gerald promised.

"Prior to her fever, did you notice any change in her memory?"

"Nothing concrete, but possibly disturbing. This morning, she was crying in her sleep…" Gerald explained what Selena had said in her feverish state.

The doctor regarded him. "I agree. Her statements are alarming."

"Yes. And it was by chance that I heard it. We both fell asleep talking…mostly about what I knew about her family, and I told her about mine. Somewhere in that, I nodded off in the chair. I woke with her crying about her father's heir hurting her, and her mother being lost. I can only imagine what horror she's gone through." Gerald felt a fresh wave of anger wash over him. And he vowed to get to the bottom of who Percival was. His father would know more. At the moment, he could do nothing but wait for his parents to arrive.

"We thought seeing her horse might spark her memory," Connery added. "Her father named the horse and had its reins embossed with a message from him and the horse's name. I thought it could provide some sentimental leverage that could help with her memory."

"That is an excellent idea," Dr. Baker replied. "Once the fever has abated, in a few days, it would be good for Miss Bowles to see her horse again. In the meantime, I'll be back later this afternoon to check on her. I know an apothecary who might have something that could prove useful to battle the infection. I'll bring it with me when I return."

"Thank you, doctor," Gerald said, shaking the older man's hand.

"Send for me immediately should anything happen. And I cannot overemphasize that she should not be left alone, given her condition," the doctor added before taking his leave.

⟫⟫⟫⟫✕⟪⟪⟪⟪

"Miss Selena, there just a few more sips of broth. Dr. Baker said it's most important that you drink it," Anna said.

"I can't… I think I've had enough," rasped Selena, leaning back against the pillow. "I feel like I've been punched in the head."

"It's the effects of the fever, miss. The doctor missed a small fragment that had burrowed into the skin," the maid replied.

"Did he reopen the wound?" Selena asked.

"Yes, Miss Selena," Anna said. "Dr. Baker will return later to see you again."

That was why her head hurt so much. What she wanted was company—specifically, she craved the viscount's company. She leaned back against the pillow. "Well, let us hope I'll be awake next time the good doctor is here, so I can turn the tables and pick his brain." She chuckled. "Oh, it hurts to laugh."

Anna smiled. "The fact that ye just made a jest means ye're a strong lass, and if you don't mind me saying, miss, that was a good quip."

"Thank you, Anna."

"Is there anything I can do for you, Miss Selena…anything?" the maid asked as she placed the empty bowl on the tray.

"Nay, thank you, Anna. You have been a dear heart."

There was a tap on the door, and Anna opened it to reveal the viscount standing in the hall. "Anna, I would like to have a few minutes with Selena. I promise not to stay long."

"Yes, milord. I'll just return the tray back to the kitchens." The young maid bobbed a curtsey and left.

When the door clicked shut, Gerald turned to her. "How are you feeling?"

"If I had a new head, I'd feel wonderful," she said.

Gerald's lips curved in a crooked smile as he sat in the chair next to the bed. Lord, even with her head throbbing and fighting a fever, she could not help her heart from thudding at his handsomeness.

"There is something I need to tell you. Something I should have told you sooner…"

"Yes?" When he hesitated, she added, "Please. You can tell me."

He reached for her hand. "Our connection is not just because our fathers were lifelong friends. We are betrothed. We've been betrothed since childhood."

A gasp escaped her. "Why did you not tell me?"

"I'm a cad. That is why. But I could no longer keep our betrothal from you."

She took a deep breath and let it out slowly. "I do not think you are a cad. My heart tells me you are not. I forgive you. But please, no more secrets?"

"I promise, no more secrets," he replied.

He lifted her hand and kissed her palm, and she felt a spark of heat that had nothing to do with her fever travel up her arm.

"When you arrived in that rainstorm and were thrown from your horse, I was shocked, alarmed, confused," he said. "But my priority was getting you inside. As I carried you up the stairs, you opened your eyes, and you recognized me and called me by name. But the next morning, you remembered nothing. Not my name, not even your own. I was worried about your condition. When I began to tell you about who you were and our families, I neglected to tell you about our betrothal because I was ashamed of how I behaved five years ago at your first London Season." Gerald told her how they first met. How she and her parents and his parents had discovered him in a compromising kiss with Lady Adamson—at her own ball, no less.

"But what I want to make clear is that everything and nothing has changed," he finished.

"Now I'm confused. Although that could be understandable, given the bump on my head."

He grinned and kissed her hand again, making her sigh. "Nothing has changed, because you are still my betrothed. But everything has changed because you are now in my care, and I will do everything in my power to make sure that you are safe. And even if you cannot remember what brought you here on that stormy night, I will find out and make sure that whoever hurt you pays for what they did."

Selena blinked back tears. Gerald was a truly kind and caring man. And she was lucky to be betrothed to him. "You have been nothing but thoughtful and kindhearted. I...sensed there was something more between us than family friendship." She gave a short laugh. "When you lose your memory, the things you learn become easier to see and understand."

"I have never thought about it like that. Kind of like having a cupboard with only one food to think about. What you will have for dinner becomes clearer, I suppose."

She laughed. "Yes, it does."

"You kissed me," he said suddenly. "Do you remember?"

She nodded slowly. "Yes. I did. It was impulsive, but I have no regrets," Selena said, quickly losing the battle to the tears filling her eyes. "I came here for a reason, and I think I came here because of you. I may not have a memory of my life, but knowing I am betrothed to a man such as you gives me hope for the future."

Gerald took out a handkerchief and gently dabbed at her cheeks, which only made more tears run down her face.

"We have not had a chance to get to know each other," he said after clearing his throat. "When you feel better, I would like to have a chance to repair that."

"I would like that too."

CHAPTER SEVEN

Two days later

SELENA AWOKE TO the warming glow of sunlight streaming in through the windows. Thank goodness—outside the window, the day appeared bright and sunny. Someone had thought to pull the curtains—it must have been Anna, that sweet maid that had been helping her.

She stretched and then winced, the movement causing her injuries to sting. She was, thankfully, feeling better each day, but she wished she could get out of bed and move around, perhaps even venture outside for some fresh air.

A light knock sounded on the door, followed by Anna's soft voice. Selena bade her enter, greeting the smiling young woman as she stepped into the room.

"Miss Selena, how do you feel this morning?" Anna asked in her lovely Scottish lilt.

"Much better, I think." She wasn't completely sure. "The fever seemed to be gone—thank goodness for that." Being alternately cold and hot—more like burning up—was no picnic. "My headache is also gone."

Anna smiled. "I'm glad to hear the headache has subsided. The fever would go, and then it would return. Several times it happened. Thank goodness it has not returned in almost a day."

"Yes, that is fortunate, indeed." Selena was thankful that Dr. Baker had discovered the source of the infection that had caused the fever and secured a tonic from the apothecary.

She had taken a liking to the pretty young maid with bright red hair, large brown eyes, and an adorable sprinkling of freckles over her nose. "Anna, do you think I might be able to take a bath today?"

"Of course, Miss Selena. I took the liberty of ordering one. The tub should be ready for you soon. But we should be careful to avoid the area around your wound."

The head wound that had caused her memory loss. Selena nodded and thanked Anna. She may have been on the mend physically, but her memory had still not returned. She couldn't even remember her name. She only knew it because *he* told her.

Gerald. Her fiancé. She'd come here to him, so that had to count for a lot, didn't it? Even though she couldn't recall why. That she had ridden through the night on a horse in a frigid rainstorm told her she was running from something. But from what? Or whom?

"Miss Selena, I washed the clothes you arrived wearing, but there were no dresses. Only another pair of britches, a shirt, and a shift and other undergarments."

"How odd." *Was I in that much of a hurry to leave?* Sorrow wrenched at her heart, and she had no idea why. There was something she should know…something she couldn't recall. She touched her head as if she could make her memory work again.

"Are you all right?" Anna asked, her brow etched in concern.

"Forgive me, Anna. It's just my frustration at my loss of memory."

"Aye. I understand," the maid said. "I have faith that your memory will return. But sometimes, some things are best forgotten." Her voice held a trace of sadness.

Selena wondered what could have caused Anna such pain that she wished she could forget it. "Sometimes, sharing a burden with someone else may lessen the load…" Now, where had she heard that before?

"Aye, perhaps you're right, miss."

"Anna, may I ask when you arrived here at Bellwood?" Perhaps there was something she could do to help the girl.

"Angus Connery is a distant cousin of mine. When Lord Bellecote hired him to oversee the property, five years ago, he brought me with him."

"Goodness! You must have been a child."

"I was but ten and two," Anna said.

That meant she was only seventeen or eighteen. So young. Anna looked to be about the same age as Selena.

However do I know that? Truth be told, she had no idea how old she was. She didn't even know what she looked like. Perhaps she would ask Gerald her age. Surely he would know.

"Do you miss your family?" she asked.

The maid blinked back sudden tears.

"I'm so sorry, Anna. I shouldn't ask such questions."

"No, miss. You have done nothing wrong. It's just that my life in Scotland wasn't the easiest. I was the…*bastard* daughter of the Earl of Kilmuir," she whispered in a broken voice. "As in England, children born on the wrong side of the blanket are not regarded and certainly not valued."

"I understand. I might not have my own memories, but somehow those harsh realities are embedded in my mind," Selena said carefully. "Forgive me for prying, but I admire your strength and courage."

"I thank ye, miss." The girl nodded. "My mother died in childbirth, so while the earl never officially claimed me, he kept me with him, hiring a nurse to take care of me. His first wife was kind and accepted me. She loved me as a mother should. She even insisted the earl provide me with a tutor so I could learn to read and write." Anna smiled as she continued, "She also taught me to sew, and other valuable skills that a lady of quality would need to know to manage a keep and a family. Aye, Lady Marian was a mother to me in my heart."

"She sounds like a wonderful woman," Selena said, feeling a lump in her throat. A great sadness enveloped her as she wondered about her own mother. And the mystery of why she would leave her behind to come here. Gerald had said he'd sent word to his father in London. Selena was most anxious to find out if he had any news.

"Aye, she was truly. I loved her so…"

"You *loved* her?" Selena reached out to grasp Anna's hand as the girl nodded, tears streaming down her cheeks.

"She died of a terrible fever while she was pregnant with the earl's child. A year later, the earl remarried. His second wife, Lady Carla, was mean and vindictive, trying to erase everything having to do with his first wife. The jealous woman became pregnant and demanded my father get me out of her sight. He reached out to Angus, who had always treated me like a loving uncle. Angus brought me here. He has always been good to me."

Selena blinked back tears. Anna's story was so heartbreaking. Even though the girl's father had not officially claimed her, he'd at least cared enough about her to keep her safe.

"Miss Selena…I almost forgot to mention. Lord Lawrence asked me to convey an invitation for a special luncheon," Anna said, a smile breaking through her tears.

Selena's heart sped up like a galloping horse. "Oh, I would be honored to attend, but…" She shook her head. "I have nothing to wear, except for the boy's clothes I had on when I arrived." She still could not fathom why she hadn't packed any clothes, not even one dress.

"I think I might be able to help you in that matter," Anna said, her eyes twinkling. "But first, would you allow me to help you out of bed?" She indicated the comfortable-looking armchair near the window.

Selena brightened at the thought, but she'd been in bed for so long that she wondered if her legs would support her if she stood. "Perhaps I should wait until Dr. Baker arrives."

"Nonsense. Lean on me," Anna said. Pulling the blankets

down, she helped ease Selena to a sitting position on the edge of the mattress. Selena placed her arm around Anna's shoulders as the maid wrapped an arm around her waist and helped her to stand. Selena's legs did feel wobbly, but she managed to stay upright as Anna helped her to the armchair next to a small, round table.

After draping a woolen shawl around Selena's shoulders, Anna excused herself and returned a few minutes later with a small blue bundle tucked under her arm. She shook it out, and Selena gasped at the lovely gown the girl held up—a sapphire-blue day dress with a pattern of small flowers in the fabric and delicate lace around the curved neckline. "It's beautiful," she breathed.

"Thank you," Anna said, beaming. "I made it myself. I purchased the muslin at the milliner's in the village. He'd acquired it from a widow last month, but no one wanted to purchase it because the fabric was several years old. As soon as I saw it, the idea for the gown came to me like a flash of lightning. The price was so affordable that I could not resist."

"Oh, Anna, the stitching is so fine," Selena said, touching the delicate seam. "You are truly gifted, but I cannot wear a dress you made for yourself."

"Oh, but I didn't make it for myself."

"Why would you make a dress you didn't plan to wear?" Selena asked.

"Remember I told you that Lady Marian, the earl's first wife, taught me to sew. She also recognized my fascination with fabric and fashioning beautiful clothing. She even took me to visit several modistes and encouraged my participation in the selection of styles for both her dresses and mine." With a somber nod, Anna added, "I owe her so much."

"What a wonderful gift you have, and what a remarkable woman Lady Marian was," Selena said softly.

"Please accept this gown as a gift, Miss Selena. And it would make me happy if you would wear it to the luncheon with Lord

Lawrence. It is perfect for you."

Selena graciously accepted the dress, feeling thankful for Anna's kindness. She vowed to herself that she would repay the maid for her generosity.

"I have the perfect hairstyle in mind," Anna said. "Let's get you bathed and dressed, and then I'll do your hair.

An hour or so later, after a relaxing bath that was most restorative, Anna began to style Selena's hair.

"There's no need to do anything elaborate, Anna. I'm only going to a luncheon…here." Selena pointed to the shaved spot on the top of her head. "And I'm not sure we can do anything short of a hat to cover this."

"Give me a chance. It may surprise you," Anna said, gently combing through Selena's chocolate-brown locks. "The viscount saw me on my way to get the dress and asked how you were doing. He wanted to make sure I had extended his invitation to you for an afternoon picnic in the garden. I agreed to escort you to him."

Selena's eyes widened at the thought of walking to the garden. It seemed so far, and she hadn't walked more than a few steps in days.

Anna handed her a looking glass and bade her look.

When Selena peeked at her reflection, she pulled back in astonishment. She looked beautiful. *Is that me?* She hadn't even given any thought to what she looked like. If someone had asked what color her eyes were, she doubted she could have answered. *I have blue eyes.* The sapphire color of the dress made her feel beautiful, despite the wound on the back of her head. She felt for the spot and realized Anna had done a masterful job camouflaging it.

"Aye, the color makes your eyes sparkle like sapphires, and the gown suits you perfectly with your coloring and dark hair. You are truly a vision, Miss Selena."

Selena hugged Anna close to her heart. "I don't have a sister, but if I had one, I'd hope she was just like you, Anna."

"I have experienced both kindness and cruelty from two ladies. Believe me when I say that kindness costs nothing. But cruelty can cost your very soul," Anna said.

CHAPTER EIGHT

G ERALD HAD LEFT nothing to chance. He wanted the picnic with Selena to be perfect. As usual, Mrs. McDonald's enthusiasm had made him smile.

"I'll prepare all yer favorites, milord," she'd said. "And I'll make my special lemon curd cake that the young miss will surely enjoy. This will be a special day, indeed!"

The cook had truly outdone herself preparing a repast of cold roast chicken, thinly sliced cold roast beef, cheese sandwiches, fresh rolls, pickled cucumbers, dried dates, and nuts—along with a variety of sliced cheeses, peach preserves with clotted cream, apple tarts, and, to drink, lemonade and wine.

Gerald put the last paint touches to the gazebo and stepped back to scrutinize his work. The transformation of the dilapidated gazebo into an elegant structure that could be enjoyed through-out the year was just one of the many changes he'd tackled over the past five years, and the result pleased him immensely.

Months ago, he had contemplated tearing it down and start-ing fresh. But he'd so admired its unique, windowed hexagon design that boasted a 360-degree view of the grounds—including an incredible variety of trees and the shimmering pond that was home to many species of waterfowl—that he decided to renovate the existing structure instead. Upon closer inspection, he'd realized that other than peeling paint, the frame was in good condition. His renovation plans included adding glass windows that would help draw in heat in the colder months and keep the rain out as well. He'd even included a modified wood stove that vented outside. He was so engrossed in thought that he didn't hear his estate manager approach.

"I'm glad you disagreed with my suggestion to tear it down," Connery said, his hands in the pockets of his jacket. "Frankly, I'm amazed at what you've done in such a short time."

Gerald smiled. "Thank you. I suppose timing is everything, as they say. The old gazebo had good bones—much of it was built with tongue and groove. It needed a second chance." Much like the second chance Bellwood had given him.

"Aye, and you've accomplished a great deal with Bellwood," Connery said, echoing his thoughts. The Scot opened the door and looked inside. "You've outdone yourself, son. Even the furnishings look as though Mother Nature herself designed them. The table is unlike anything I've ever seen—a wooden table intentionally painted white and then weathered to look old."

"I owe that to Anna and Mrs. Evans. It seems the two of them have hidden decorating talents. They found the old, discarded table in the attic. Mrs. Evans decided a white table that appeared aged would be appealing and easier to maintain in the gazebo. It was sanded and painted and then..." Gerald scratched his head. "She said she used a dry brush to age it."

"I've never seen that before, but I like it. The pastel-blue ladder chairs are also a nice touch," Connery added.

"Yes. I was unsure of her directions, but since I invited her to help me, I let her do what she wanted, thinking I could always change it. She decided plump cushions would make the chairs comfortable, and they could be stored inside the house. Anna thinks the whole effect, especially with the crystal and lace tablecloth, is enchanting." Gerald grinned. "Speaking of looking enchanting, I better head back to wash and change before Selena arrives." He held up his paint-stained hands.

"I'll get out of your way," Connery said with a wink. "Save

me an apple tart."

Gerald chuckled as he withdrew his pocket watch and checked the time. In two hours, Anna would escort Selena to the gazebo. And then he would tell her everything...

GERALD COULD HAVE rivaled his prized racehorse Aphrodite in his rush to bathe and change for his lunch with Selena. He'd rushed back just as Mrs. McDonald and Mrs. Evans were finished setting the table and laying out the platters and plates of food. He thanked the two older women with kisses on their cheeks. They fussed over him and made sure his cravat was perfect.

Mrs. McDonald and Mrs. Evans were like two dear aunts who had not only supported him but taught him a great deal about the domestic side of running an estate. He was glad of that knowledge, and everything else he'd learned over the years, all part and parcel of his leaving his youthful indiscretions behind and taking control of his life. He'd need to rely on everything he'd learned to tell Selena what he needed to say.

His stomach churned with anxiety over the significance of today's lunch. It was a pivotal moment, and he was determined to make amends for his past behavior toward his betrothed. Had he not been so preoccupied with his resentment toward his father for arranging the engagement when they were children, he might have recognized the preciousness of Selena's presence sooner. Despite his inner turmoil, he managed to make it back well before Anna escorted Selena to the gazebo.

Gerald perused the bounty of dishes on the long table set against one wall of the gazebo. He hadn't known what to ask Mrs. McDonald to prepare. Given Selena's amnesia, he couldn't ask her what she liked. But the cook felt sure the menu of his favorites would please his betrothed. He hoped she was right. He then turned to admire the dining table. Mrs. Evans had outdone herself by creating a rustic centerpiece of wildflowers, juxtaposed by elegant china and delicate crystal glassware.

He rubbed his hands together in anticipation. He had just enough time to light the wood stove before Selena arrived.

Closing the stove, he heard soft, feminine laughter and stepped outside to watch as Selena and Anna approached. His breath caught as he beheld Selena's striking beauty. How could he have not seen the promise of who she'd become? He'd been such a buffoon. He realized it was because he had been searching for every reason not to like her. He had gone out of his way to spoil anything related to their engagement, including ruining her Society debut.

Shame tightened his chest as he remembered what Selena had witnessed in the Adamsons' garden that night five years ago. Lady Adamson's bruised lips and disheveled appearance had left little to the imagination. Even though his rendezvous with her had been part of a stupid bet with his friends, Gerald realized there had been a darker reason for that night and all his shenanigans back then. He'd known he could be discovered, but he'd been driven to take that risk to punish his father for betrothing him to a woman not of his choosing. All he could focus on was undermining everything that his father had taught him, while completely disregarding the feelings and needs of an innocent sixteen-year-old girl who had essentially been placed in the same situation as him, through no fault of her own. Not only did he need to apologize to Selena, but he also had to atone for his horrendous behavior.

Selena widened her eyes and beamed. "What an enchanting place," she said with a soft gasp.

"Aye, truly enchanting," Anna said, exchanging a wink with Gerald.

"Thank you, ladies," he said. He was having trouble holding on to a thought as he beheld his betrothed. "You look lovely, Selena."

"Thank you," she breathed, blushing prettily. "Anna created

this lovely gown for me."

"You have a true gift, Anna," he said. Gerald made a mental note to compensate the maid for her fine work. The gown could rival any London modiste.

"Thank you, milord. Enjoy your picnic." Anna grinned, dipping a curtsey before withdrawing.

Gerald turned back to Selena. He could not help admiring how the blue floral print gown enhanced the color of her eyes. "You are a vision."

"Thank you, my lord." Selena blushed again.

How he loved making her blush.

She smoothed the skirt of her gown. "I think I owe it all to this gown—it's as lovely as anything I've ever owned."

"Anything you ever owned?" he repeated.

Selena looked stunned. "I...I don't know what made me say that. Do you think perhaps my memory is returning?"

"I pray it is so," he said, taking his hand in hers. "You don't know what stirred you to say that?"

"I think I must favor blue. Perhaps that could be it," she said, worrying her lower lip.

He tucked her arm through his. "Your memory will return. I am sure of it." And when it did, he would find out what Percival Bowles had done to her. And make him pay.

Gerald helped her up the low steps into the gazebo.

"Oh, how lovely," Selena said as she turned in a slow circle, taking in the interior. "'Tis even more magical inside." Her gaze met his. "You did all of this for our picnic?"

Gerald nodded. "Come, let us enjoy our feast."

They walked to the food table, and Selena gasped at the array of dishes.

"Oh, my!" she said. "The food looks scrumptious. How could you have known lemon cake is my favorite?" She shot a surprised look at him. "Wait... How did *I* know that? What if I *am* getting my memory back?"

A smile curved his mouth. "I am sure of it," Gerald said. A

wave of guilt washed over him. If her memory returned, she would recall how callously he'd behaved toward her the night of her debut.

He needed to tell her the truth about that night. He hoped she would still look at him the way she was now.

Gerald handed Selena a plate and assisted with her selections. He was pleased that she wanted a little of everything. It was no surprise, considering she'd only had broth for days. Her appetite was an indication she was on the mend. She was no shy miss about eating what appealed to her, and he loved that.

He carried their plates to their table and held her chair for her.

After sitting, she took a sip of wine and glanced back at the buffet.

"Is everything all right?" he asked.

She leaned in and whispered, "That lemon cake really does look tempting. Would you think badly of me if I ate that first?" she asked. "I want to be certain I have room for it."

He answered with a soft laugh. "No, I don't mind at all. It happens to be my favorite as well. Honestly, I love the idea." He got up and retrieved two slices of cake.

"I'll pass on the other sweets for now," she said before tucking into the lemony dessert.

Her tongue flicked over her lips, and he found himself mesmerized. Realizing he was staring, he forced his attention to his plate.

Get a hold of yourself, man—you're not some schoolboy nursing a first crush. Perhaps this would be a good time to apologize to her, he thought. His behavior in a different gazebo five years ago hung like a cloud over his head, and he would like nothing better than to move past it.

Just as he was about to apologize, a sudden shower caught them both by surprise, considering it was still sunny.

He stood and helped her to the door, instinctively knowing she would appreciate the sight of the sun shower. He unlatched the door and opened the top half.

Selena took a deep breath of the rain-filled air. "How beautiful… Everything is glowing. Rain showers make everything smell so fresh." He watched her face as she gazed at the view outside the gazebo. "Look how the sun is pushing through the rain, almost as if they are trying to outdo each other."

Was the sudden shower some sort of sign that he should wait to apologize? Its timing had created almost a divine diversion. But while he was usually happy for any diversion, the sun shower actually seemed a good sign that he *should* tell her.

"There is something I'd like to talk to you about, Selena. Something important." He helped her back to her seat.

"What is it you need to tell me, Gerald?" She smiled, giving him her full attention. She was straightforward and guileless—something else he liked about her.

His stomach churned nervously. "I'd like to apologize to you," he began.

"Apologize?" She arched a delicate brow. "You have been nothing but kind since I arrived here," she said. "You saved my life. I feel safe with you."

Her openly adoring gaze took his breath away. *God, I was such a heel.* Despite that, he forged forward.

"You are perfectly safe—however, I have not always been kind. The last time we saw each other was five years ago. At the time, I was not ready to marry and rebelled against my parents over my forced betrothal. Unfortunately, I did that without giving any thought to how my actions would make you feel. That night we were to meet in person, for the first time since we were children, was at the Adamsons' ball. Despite our betrothal, we were virtual strangers. Which was why our parents had wanted us to meet. You were sixteen, attending with your parents. It was your first London Season. But that same night, I'd made a bet with my friends. A stupid bet. We bet how long it would take Lady Adamson to proposition each of us."

A flush infused Selena's cheeks, but she nodded for him to

continue.

"Lady Adamson was thirty years younger than her husband and, quite frankly, well known for her various liaisons. That night, I won the bet. And the prize was a rendezvous in Adamson's garden at the ball. At the same time, my parents and your parents and you were taking a stroll through the gardens…"

Selena's eyes widened. "Oh… I see."

Gerald nodded. "We were discovered. My parents, your parents, and you came upon Lady Adamson and me engaged in a rather animated embrace in a gazebo."

"A gazebo…"

"At the time, I froze. I looked at you and you were so young, so innocent. But I was too selfish, too rebellious, too immature…" His face felt hot. For the first time in his life, Gerald realized what real shame felt like. "I should have apologized to you and your parents back then. In person and in writing. But I didn't—I was a cad and a scoundrel. It was only when my father banished me here"—he spread his arms, gesturing around him—"that I began to grow up and become the kind of man who I hope is worthy of you.

"I deeply regret my actions—for embarrassing my family and causing insult to yours. But most of all, I am so sorry for hurting you." He looked into her beautiful eyes, now shimmering with tears. "I hope you can forgive me," he said in a hoarse voice. "I hope you will allow me to atone for my past, and I hope you will continue to accept me as your betrothed…"

Selena listened and remained silent for a while after he finished speaking. Finally, she took a deep breath and released it slowly. "While I agree that you were selfish and brash, and hurtful, I am thankful for your honesty with me today," she said in a husky voice, her eyes brimming with tears. "And I believe you have spent a long time thinking about your past and changing your life." She reached out and laid her hand over his. "You have opened your home and your heart to me. I may not have my memory, but I have a sound mind. And I see a good man before me. A man who is respected and beloved by everyone who works for him. A man who sat by my bedside all night and cared for me through my fever. I see a man who has gone to so much effort to please me. I don't think our futures should be defined by mistakes we made in the past. Even though I cannot remember that night, I believe that should my memory return, I will feel the same as I do right now. I forgive you, Gerald."

My God, she is incredible. He didn't deserve to be betrothed to her, but he would do his damndest to make sure he never hurt her again. "Selena, I just want—"

"Hush." She smiled, placing her finger on his lips. "No more apologies. You are forgiven." Then she looked up at him. "I want to know more about you, Viscount Lawrence…the man you are today. That is what is important to me. Now, tell me more about this lovely estate that you have worked so hard to renovate. What do you love the most about the work you do here? What are your goals for the future? What do you enjoy doing most in life? Tell me anything and everything. With my memory gone, I'm still trying to figure that out about myself, although I think it has something to do with the outdoors. But it's my sincere hope that we can have something we enjoy in common."

Gerald slanted his head and looked at this beautiful woman across from him. He was certain most women would have slapped him across the face and walked away from him, but not this one. Instead, she had given him grace. What mattered to Selena was the here and now. This slip of a girl who couldn't remember her past. Perhaps that was what should matter. In just a matter of days, Selena Bowles had completely upended his life. She was the most incredible woman he'd ever met. His anxiety had calmed, and his heart felt lighter.

"Horses," he answered.

"Tell me about your racehorses," she said. "They are such noble and kind animals, I should think it would be most exhilarating to watch them race."

"More than you can imagine," he said. "One day I'll take you.

And they are, indeed, noble."

"Have you won any races?"

"I have." He grinned. "When my father banished me here, he essentially challenged me to do something useful with my life. I was resentful at first, but then I realized he was right, and so I set out to meet his challenge and hopefully build something I could be proud of…and that perhaps would make him proud of me too. Over time, and with Connery's guidance and wisdom, I learned a lot about raising thoroughbreds and racing them. I suppose you could say I developed a passion for it."

"I am certain your father is proud of you," she said softly.

Gerald swallowed the lump in his throat as he gazed at her lovely face.

"I would love to meet all of your horses—" Selena's eyes suddenly widened at something over his shoulder.

"Is everything all right?"

"Yes, something is quite wonderful," she said, pointing to the pond beyond the window. "A pair of swans, Gerald. May we take a closer look?"

"Of course." Grinning at her enthusiasm, he stood and took her hand, helped her up, and escorted her out to the pond. The grass was damp, but not muddy, given the rain had stopped and the sun was warm.

The swans glided side by side, leaving a slight ripple in the surface of the water. The symbolism of the pair didn't escape him. Swans mated for life, and the duo in the pond appeared to have built their nest nearby.

Selena turned to Gerald, her face aglow. "Isn't it the most beautiful sight you've ever seen?"

"*You're* the most beautiful sight I've ever seen," he whispered. He tipped her chin up and slowly lowered his mouth to hers. Her lips were soft—almost silky against his own. A sweet sigh escaped her as he deepened the kiss. He could feel the soft tickle of her breath beneath his nose as he twined the tips of his fingers in the loose, dark curls framing her face. In that moment, time stood still.

CHAPTER NINE

The next morning

THE SUN PEEKING through the sheer lace curtains awakened Selena. Stretching, she leaned back and looked at the prisms of color beaming through the clear, leaded cathedral-glass transoms above the windows on the wall opposite her bed. The blue of the sky signaled a clear day, one without rain. Although the sun shower yesterday had been perfect.

Smiling, she leaned back and reflected on her picnic luncheon with Gerald—his heartfelt apology, the unexpected shower, the swans, and...that kiss. She had dreamed about that kiss. The touch of his lips sent small quivers of pleasure up her back. Her instincts told her she'd never experienced those feelings before.

Her heart was aflutter at the thought of seeing Gerald again. He'd said he would see her today, and weather permitting, they might take a walk. He'd also mentioned something about a surprise. She could not help the excitement bubbling inside her. Even though she still hadn't reclaimed her memories, she was feeling hopeful about the future. She'd been so ill and was only just starting to feel stronger, but she also needed to talk to Gerald about her mother. He'd sent a missive to his parents and his friend Asher informing them of the situation and was certain they would have answers for her when they arrived. She prayed her mother was safe, but she couldn't help but wonder and worry about what had happened. She still didn't know the reason she'd ridden to Gerald's estate.

The door opened and Anna entered carrying a breakfast tray, a beautiful dark pink muslin dress over her arm. "Good morning, Miss Selena. I brought you some chocolate and biscuits." She set the tray down on the table next to Selena's bed.

"Good morning, Anna. Thank you. Isn't it just the most glorious day?"

"If you're referring to the sunshine and blue skies, then I agree." Anna grinned. "What are your plans for the day?"

"I'm not sure. Gerald mentioned that he might have a surprise for me. Perhaps a walk…" Selena took a sip of the chocolate and closed her eyes in bliss. "What a lovely gown you have there," she said, indicating the dress Anna laid on the bed.

"It's for you, miss. I made it from an older dress of pink muslin that I found in a trunk in the attic. Mrs. Evans said it would be fine for me to alter. I think it must have belonged to the former mistress of the house…before Lord Lawrence arrived. It's a day dress, and I'm anxious to see it on you."

"It's beautiful. Thank you for your generosity. That shade of pink is so rich and pretty. Almost a rose pink." Selena reached out and touched it. "It's exquisite. And the delicate floral embroidery is so lovely… Do you know what kind of flowers those are? The name seems to have escaped me."

"They are pansies, miss. They are very popular around here in the colder weather—as long as the rabbits and deer don't get to them." Anna chuckled. "That used to happen at home quite regularly."

"I suppose they like to eat, too." Selena winked. "I can understand how that might frustrate a gardener, though. I thank you again for this beautiful dress. You are as generous as you are talented, Anna."

The maid gave a shy smile and placed the dress on the back of a nearby chair. "I am happy to help. We were so worried when you developed a fever. Thank goodness Dr. Baker was able to find the reason for the infection. Are you feeling better today?"

"Yes, each day I feel a bit stronger. I imagine I'll be prone to headaches for a while."

"Aye, I can imagine that, but I'm pleased you are feeling stronger. Do you feel up to a bath today?

"I would love a bath," Selena said. "Would you be able to style my hair?"

"Of course." The young maid nodded. "I'll wash and bandage the wound first and then style your hair. I promise to hide the bandage."

"You're so good to me, Anna. Thank you," Selena said. "As I said, Gerald mentioned that we might go for a walk later. However, I'd very much like to spend time with my horse this morning. Would you be able to accompany me?"

"I'd be happy to escort you to the stables. Mrs. Evans has a few things she needs me to do today, so I will escort you and then return to get you later. Will that be all right?"

"Yes, I think so. I feel much better on my feet. There's no dizziness. I promise I will take it slow and not overtax myself," Selena said.

An hour later, she was dressed in her new day gown. Despite not having regained her memory, she felt better physically, and her heart was still full of joy from yesterday. And she was also looking forward to visiting with Azure.

Selena and Anna left the manor house and headed toward the stables. When they walked inside, the stables seemed quiet.

"Are you sure you feel comfortable here, miss?" Anna asked. "I don't feel good about leaving you on your own."

"She won't be here on her own, Anna," a young boy said, coming out from a stall carrying a bucket of feed.

"Joshua. I'm glad you are here. Have you met Miss Selena?" Anna said.

"No, but I have met her beautiful stallion, Azure. I just brushed him down and gave him some oats. He'll be very happy to see her," Joshua said.

"Would you take me? That's why I'm here," Selena said.

"I'm getting ready to brush Aphrodite and Athena. He's on my way, miss. I'd be glad to take you," the boy said.

"Thank you, Joshua," Anna said. "I best be getting back to the house to help Mrs. Evans."

"I'll be all right," Selena said, playfully shooing the maid out of the stables.

"Miss Selena, your horse is just a few stalls down on the right. I'll take you there," Joshua said.

"You've got your arms full. I don't want to hold you up. You go and I'll follow."

"If you wish," the young boy said before going on his way.

Selena stood there for a few moments, admiring the renovated stables. Large lanterns hung on the walls, lighting a corridor full of oaken-stained wooden stalls. She noticed one next to her looked larger than the rest and wondered if that was for a foaling mare or a sick horse. The floors were cobbled and had shallow drainage channels that ran alongside the stalls. Above her, thick beams supported a high-pitched roof. She thought it was a large, beautiful stable, even if she could remember nothing to compare it to. Selena hoped to ask Gerald to introduce her to his racehorses.

As she started to make her way down the aisle, she heard a large kick, followed by neighing and whinnying. It sounded like an agitated horse was nearby. Her curiosity got the better of her, and she followed the noise to a large black stallion who threw another kick at the side of the stall and began pawing the straw in front of him.

As she approached, he snorted and shook his head. Hanging on to a metal bar, she climbed up on the gate and leaned over. The horse moved toward her, nostrils flaring.

"Hello, my beauty," she said softly. The horse blew through his nostrils and laid his head on Selena's shoulder. She held on to the metal bar with one hand and reached out to gently touch the side of his neck with the other, making gentle circles. "You look so sad. What's wrong, sweet baby?" she whispered.

"Climb down and move away, Selena. You could be hurt."

Selena glanced over her shoulder, and before she could blink, Gerald had lifted her down and drawn her into his arms. "The horse might have lashed out at you," he whispered.

Moved by Gerald's action, she blinked back sudden tears. "Thank you for being so protective of me, but I was in no danger from this lovely creature." She couldn't help but love the feel of his strong arms around her. His masculine scent of sandalwood and citrus made her feel like swooning, but for good reasons.

He released her and stepped back. "I'm sorry I was worried when I saw you petting Apollo. He's been volatile lately."

"I understand," she said. "But as you can see, he is very gentle." She reached up and rubbed the horse above his nose. "You'll be right as rain, won't you, my beauty?" she whispered gently. The stallion nickered softly in reply.

"My God, I haven't seen that in a long time," Connery said, walking up to them.

"What do you mean?" Gerald asked.

"Apollo has been acting out for the past two weeks. And this lass here whispered a few words and petted his nose, and he's as docile as a lamb." Connery turned to Selena with a grin. "Ye have a special gift, Miss Bowles. The last time I saw anything similar was when I was a young man in Scotland. The villagers called the woman a witch."

Selena felt a blush suffuse her cheeks. "I don't think I have a gift. I do love animals, though. I don't know how I know that, but I just do."

"Can you sense what's wrong with the stallion?" Connery asked.

Selena turned back to the thoroughbred and gently rubbed his face. In response, he blew softly from his nostrils. "Has this horse been taken recently from its maman?" she asked over her shoulder.

Gerald and Connery exchanged a glance.

"Yes, as a matter of fact," Gerald said. "We purchased him a couple of weeks ago. His mother is still at the breeder's estate. Why do you ask?"

"Because I think he's missing his mother. If you bring her here for a visit, I think he will calm down. Horses, like people, have a close bond with their mothers."

"That's remarkable," Gerald said. "You're remarkable..."

"Th-thank you, my lord." Her eyes met his and she felt faint, but not from fever—from the intensity of his gaze.

"As I said, 'tis a rare gift ye have there, Miss Bowles," Connery said.

A dog gave a loud bark and trotted up to them. "Hello, friend." She smiled and, crouching down, petted the animal's shaggy white head. "You look familiar. Have we met before?" She giggled as the dog licked her nose.

"That's Dutch. He's a shameless flirt," Gerald said dryly. "When you arrived during the storm, he was spooked by the lightning and thought you and Azure were a threat—he ran up to you barking and startled Azure, who reared up, and that led to your fall."

"Ah. So, you are feeling guilty, you handsome boy," Selena said, giving him another rub on his head and back. Dutch sat, then lifted his paw and rested it on her knee.

"I've never seen him react to anyone like that," commented Gerald. "It appears he seems to be asking for forgiveness. He's typically more reserved and waits until he gets to know people before he shows affection."

"You didn't mean to cause me pain, Dutch," Selena said soothingly. "So there's nothing to forgive."

Dutch thumped his tail and gave a soft woof.

"I see your gift is not limited to horses," Connery said, chuckling.

"I don't think it's a gift. I think he responds to a friendly voice." She smiled and accepted Gerald's hand as he helped her stand. "May I see Azure? My original purpose for coming here was to spend some time with him."

"Of course." He escorted her to the stall at the end of the aisle, nearest the other entrance. "He's a fine steed."

"How beautiful he is." Selena approached the large gray stallion who stood with a calm nobility. "Hello, Azure," she said softly, reaching up to pet his nose. The horse blew air and moved his head as though he were nodding to her, welcoming her back. "May I go into the stall? I don't think he will hurt me." Something drove her to get closer to the horse, and standing over the gate seemed too far.

The gray horse whinnied and nodded again.

Gerald smiled. "It looks like I'm outnumbered. I'll stay outside the stall, in case you need me."

"Thank you," she said, closing the stall's gate behind her.

A pain in her chest told her she had missed this horse something fierce. "You look wonderful." She petted his nose and then, reaching up, wrapped her arms around his neck, placing her head against his. "Thank you for getting me here safely. I'm feeling much better."

The horse nuzzled her neck with his nose.

"I believe Azure just kissed you. Should I be jealous?" Gerald teased.

Beaming, she turned and faced her fiancé. "It feels familiar, so I think he always does that with me. Thank you for taking such good care of my sweet Azure. I have missed spending time with him."

"How do you know...that you have missed him?" Gerald asked. "Are you remembering?"

She thought for a moment. "I can't remember details, but feelings, yes. I think I can remember feeling close to Azure. Safe. Protected..."

Dutch crouched down and slid beneath the gate of the stall. Selena smiled and noticed Azure seemed to accept him. The dog rose and stood next to Selena and nudged her skirts. She leaned down and kissed the large white creature on the head.

Connery joined them. "I think I've seen it all now. The dog appears to have sought forgiveness from the horse as well."

"It appears so," Gerald said, chuckling.

"That might explain why he's been sleeping close to your horse's stall these last few nights," Connery said. "Joshua told me the dog had moved his nightly post to the front of this stall."

"Is there any animal you cannot tame?" Gerald asked.

"They have become friends," Selena said. As she stood there, her horse began to nuzzle her neck and paw at the ground. She leaned in and wrapped her arm around his mane. As Azure calmed, she looked into his eyes and whispered, "What is it, boy?"

The horse whimpered and shook his head, then looked in the direction of the stall they had come from.

"He seems to want to know about the other horse," she said. "Azure seems concerned about him."

"Most unusual," Connery commented.

Selena kissed Azure's nose. "The horse missed his mother," she whispered. As she answered him, her head began to throb—a merciless pain that rose from behind her skull to her forehead.

"Are you all right?" Gerald asked, moving into the stall and stepping beside her. "Selena, please answer me…"

She could hear voices in her head. *"Darlings."* She recognized her father. *"He is a good and honorable young man. His father, Arthur, and I were cousins and friends when we were young. Percival will take good care of you."*

The voices grew loud and angry… Strangers in her home…saying horrible things to her… *"Your mother is dead… She succumbed to her fever,"* one stranger said. He was ugly, with greasy black hair and foul, whisky-tinged breath. His voice was cold and harsh.

"No! It's not true. Please, take me to her now."

"I am your guardian, and you will obey me… Be ready to depart right after your mother's funeral tomorrow. We will be traveling to Gretna Green. For our wedding." He gave her a leering grin as he

dragged her against him, bruising her mouth in a slobbering kiss...

Tears streamed down her face, and she began to scream.

She could hear Gerald calling to her, but he was so far away.

I have to get to Gerald... Gerald, help me...

He...he killed my mother...

As everything began to spin, she felt herself falling into some kind of dark abyss. She could hear his evil laugh. She heard Gerald call to her, but he was fading. Darkness was descending. But she had to find her mother and reach Gerald before he was too far. The roaring increased in her ears, becoming louder until she cried out in desperation. Gripping her head, she heard herself scream before everything went black.

CHAPTER TEN

Rose Point Chateau
Nottingham, England
That same day

"GROM, GET THE hell in here."

"Yes, my lord," the lumbering giant of a man said in his usual guttural monotone.

"What do you mean you've spoken to *everyone*, and *no one* has any information on them? Liars, all of them! The first thing I'm going to do when I return from my wedding trip is raise the rent on all their properties. They'll know I mean business when I ask for their help. *Someone knows something!*" Vern bellowed.

"They know nothing. And I believe them," Grom countered.

"It's *my lord*. I am Lord Percival Bowles. You address me as *my lord*. Do you understand?"

"My lord, they know nothing. And I found nothing to make me believe otherwise. If you take out your vengeance on the people in the village, your coffers will dry up," Grom said. "Then your ruse as Lord Bowles will dry up."

"Nonsense! They are wastrels and have nowhere to go," Vern spewed. But he worried Grom may have a point.

"As you say, my lord," the hulking man said.

Suddenly, the room felt smaller, as if the walls were closing in on Vern. No one was doing as he said. He needed to show them he meant it, but first, he would find the girl. He had dreamed about that girl, and he would have her.

"We must find her. What did she take?" Vern demanded. It couldn't have been anything of value. He'd had everything he could find of worth taken from her room.

"We searched the room before locking her in there, so she had nothing of value," Grom replied.

"Except her horse," Vern muttered. "And a resourceful young woman would have saved some coin. Search every nook and cranny. Send a maid to her room to search and have them bring me whatever they find. You've questioned the cook's helper and the stable helpers?"

"I have. They saw nothing."

"They had to have seen *something*. They're just not talking," Vern groused.

"They are loyal to no one, my lord. I offered them coin for answers, but they had nothing."

"I see. And this coin you offered…where were you planning to get it?"

Grom stared at him with such intensity, it caused Vern to flinch.

"All right. You have a share of whatever we take. That was the agreement. You have nothing to worry about. I'm good for it."

"I have everything to worry about," Grom said. "You've killed her ma, killed her cousin and taken his place, and now you can't be satisfied until you marry her—and I don't see that happening easily, with witnesses. None of that was what we discussed. If you don't leave well enough alone, we're going to dangle at the end of a rope. Her father was one of them real lords, with hoity-toity people in high places."

Feeling a strange heat on his neck, Vern nodded. "Let me know if anyone finds anything."

Vern returned to Bowles's study—which was now *his* study—and stared. *Where should I begin?* He'd heard of secret hiding places in these studies. Perhaps the old viscount had installed one. Walking to the bookcase, he looked at the shelves at eye level and began pulling out tomes and tossing them to the floor. Nothing. He started on the shelf below it and repeated the process. Still nothing. He could do this all day and not find a thing.

Moving quickly to the large oak desk, he unlocked it and pulled out the center drawer. Seeing nothing, he flung it to the ground. Pulling out the large drawers one by one, he searched the contents. He paused at the drawer that contained his stock of brandy. There were *no* plans to toss that onto the floor. With-drawing an almost empty flask, he emptied it into his cup before pulling another fresh bottle from the wood cabinet near his desk and topping his glass. "Her father had good taste in whisky. I'll give him that," he muttered to himself.

The door opened, and Grom entered.

Vern started to snap at the man, but remembered himself. Grom had reminded him of their bargain, and while he planned to usurp the other man's fortune, he needed him at this moment. Pasting a placid look on his face, he asked, "Did you have any luck?"

"No, my lord. Nothing. She left the dress she had worn before taking to her bed, and the maid commented you had ordered her armoire cleaned out before you locked her in the room. I'm not sure what she could be wearing."

"I'm sure you want to know what I'm doing. I'm trying to find something…anything at all that will tell us where she went, or where the cook and her husband went. If we find one, we will most likely find the other," Vern said.

"Have you checked under the desk?" Grom asked, pointing.

"Of course I—" Vern stopped. "No." He dropped down and crawled under, moving the drawers back and forth. "There is a panel behind this drawer. It's a false back." He slid the drawer out and pulled out the panel. A pile of neatly arranged papers spilled out. Vern snatched them up and threw them on the top of his desk. "Don't just stand there…start looking with me."

Grom moved to the desk, and the two men scoured the papers. At last, Vern pushed back and shook a folded document in his hand. "I think this could be it." Spreading the document out on his desk, he read it, mumbling as he went along. "Aha! It's that betrothal document her mother mentioned. Better than that...it gives the London address for the betrothed! Pack your bags. We leave in an hour, and we have a lot to do."

"Yes, my lord," Grom said as he took his leave.

Vern remembered Selena's mother mentioning the lord's name, but he had been enjoying his brandy at dinner that night and didn't ask to see proof. With the mother out of the way, he had forgotten all about the betrothal.

Vern laughed maniacally and waved the papers in the air. Selena's crafty mother had withheld information about a very rich inheritance. Names were one thing, but it wouldn't have mattered how much alcohol he consumed—he would never have forgotten *that* juicy tidbit of information. He tapped the betrothal document in the palm of his other hand. With the information this record provided, he could set himself up comfortably.

I will find the girl. Surely she would have sought refuge with this man's family, as there was no other family he knew of to help her. He would find out where that bastard lived, and he would put an end to the pesky problem. Now that he knew *who* her intended was, it should be easy to find her. And when he did, he planned to ensure the interloper posed no further threat. Once that was taken care of, they would take a trip to Gretna Green. After that, he would claim a dowry—almost legitimately—and any other money she had coming, including the sale of all unentailed possessions.

But first, he would enjoy her company and all she offered. After obtaining all the money, Vern planned to leave for Spain. There was a certain barmaid there that he missed.

Bellwood Estate
Derbyshire, England

"CALL DR. BAKER now," Gerald said, rushing upstairs, holding Selena, followed by Dutch and Connery. What had happened to her? She had clearly been in pain—her head—before dropping into a dead faint.

"Right away, my lord," Wells said from behind him.

"Have Anna and Mrs. Evans meet us upstairs," Gerald said, taking the stairs two at a time to reach the parlor.

He pushed open the door and laid her on the settee. Grabbing a chair, he pulled it next to the bed. She was so still. He leaned over her face to feel her breath. *Thank God!*

Mrs. Evans and Anna rushed in behind him. "What happened, my lord?" the housekeeper asked.

He struggled to push the lump from his throat. *What if I've lost her...just when I found her?* "I'm not sure. She gripped her head, as if it pained her tremendously, screamed, and then...fainted."

The housekeeper uncorked a small vial. Gently lifting Selena's head, she waved the smelling salts beneath her nose. "Come on, child. Wake up." As Selena stirred, her hands thrashed above her, until Mrs. Evans gently took them and held them in hers. "Selena, darlin' girl...wake up."

Selena opened her eyes. Her face was ashen. Trembling, she looked at Mrs. Evans and then over at Gerald. Her eyes filled with tears, and she began to sob. "He killed her. He killed my mother," she wept. "My mother is gone...and he wouldn't let me see her. He poisoned her. I know he did."

Gerald pulled her up into his arms and held her against his chest. "Who killed her, Selena?" he whispered.

"Percival...my cousin Percival killed her. He's a m...monster," she hiccupped.

"No, he didn't," a woman's voice said from the entrance to the parlor.

CHAPTER ELEVEN

GERALD SWIVELED HIS head toward the doorway to see Lady Fleur Bowles standing there alongside his father and mother, Lord and Lady Bellecote. Behind them stood his best friend, Lord Asher Wright, and the rest of his family—his brother-in-law Christopher Anglesey, the Marquess of Banbury, with his wife, his sister Diana, as well as his youngest sister, Gabby. Gerald immediately recalled the invitations to celebrate the holiday at his estate. He had forgotten about the holidays and realized he hadn't done a thing toward readying the estate for the festivities. Selena's unexpected arrival had consumed his thoughts. But with Diana and his mother here, he was sure that they could easily remedy the situation.

"Maman!" Selena tried to get up, but Gerald stayed her with his hand.

"Selena, love, you just dropped in a dead faint, screaming in pain, in the stables. You could have reinjured your head. Let your mother come to you," he said softly.

He helped Selena to sit up as her mother rushed forward to embrace her daughter.

"How…? What happened, Maman?" she cried as she clung to her mother.

"*Ma chérie,*" her mother said, pulling her daughter to her breast.

Needing answers and, at the same time, wanting to crush the head of Percival Bowles, Gerald approached his family and greeted them.

Wells appeared at the door. "My lord, Dr. Baker—" Before he could finish, the doctor strode into the room.

Gerald quickly explained the situation and introduced him to Selena's mother. After asking Anna to remain in the parlor to assist, Gerald ushered his family into the drawing room to tell them everything that had happened in the past few days. Connery excused himself and said he would be in the stables. Mrs. Evans returned a short while later with Rosie, one of the kitchen maids, pushing a tea cart with refreshments.

Gerald wanted to ask his parents to tell him everything, but he could not do that in front of his infant niece and nephew, nor Gabby.

"The rooms are all prepared," Mrs. Evans announced as she withdrew from the room.

"Please don't think badly of me, sweet brother," Diana said. "But these babies are tired and need to be fed."

"Son, we all need to get a good night's sleep, including you," his father added. "Tomorrow morning will be soon enough for us to talk about everything that has happened. Everyone is safe and sound, and that is the important thing."

Gerald nodded, even though he knew he would get no sleep tonight.

Gabby rushed over and gave him a quick hug. "I'm so sorry about all the horrid things that have happened. But I'm so glad we're here. The house looks wonderful. I cannot wait to see everything…everywhere," she said, lifting on her toes and kissing her brother.

"I'm glad too, Gabby." Gerald hugged her tightly. "I'll see you all tomorrow morning—have a good night's sleep."

GERALD MADE HIS way to the parlor. Just as he was about to knock on the door, Dr. Baker opened it.

"I was just about to call for a footman to get you," the doctor said.

"How is she?"

"Much better. Perhaps we could speak in private?"

"Yes, of course." Gerald led the way to this study and offered the doctor a seat.

"It appears she has regained her memory. I'm not sure what prompted the change, and it's hard to say definitively that *all* her memories have returned, but it seems so," Dr. Baker said.

"Is she all right?" Gerald asked.

"I gave her a sedative to help her sleep through the night. It is for the best that she rests."

After the doctor had finished filling Gerald in on Selena's condition, Gerald thanked him and escorted him to the door.

"You're welcome, of course. I've got a birth to get to. But send for me if anything changes. I'll be at Mrs. Whitton's. Miss Bowles has had a terrible shock," he said. "She needs to stay as calm as possible. Although, considering she hasn't seen her mother in some time, it seems unlikely.

"Thank you, Dr. Baker," Gerald said.

Gerald returned to the parlor feeling a curious mixture of relieved, concerned, and saddened to see Selena sedated on the couch. "Lady Bowles, I realized that I never properly welcomed you to Bellwood. We are very happy you are here." He looked down at the sleeping Selena. "She needed you, and the timing of your arrival was perfect."

The woman swiped at a tear that leaked from her eye. "I am glad I arrived when I did," Lady Bowles said, gently running her hand over her daughter's forehead, pushing back a few strands of damp hair. "I missed my sweet daughter so much."

"Selena is an amazing young woman. And I have benefited from the time this has given me to get to know her. I've found her to be a very determined, strong, and brave woman. I have come to care for her very much," he said.

"That makes me happy. Phillip and I argued when he first brought up the idea of a betrothal. But he felt so strongly about it, even though we both wanted her to marry someone who would love her."

She looked down at her daughter, and it seemed to Gerald that there was more she wanted to say about that.

Instead, she looked up and smiled. "Thank you, Lord Lawrence, for taking care of my little girl."

"I will take her to her room."

He lifted Selena and carried her upstairs, gently placing her on her bed. Her mother tucked her in and kissed her forehead. As he turned to leave the room, her maid entered. "Anna, please escort Lady Bowles to her room."

"If you don't mind, Lord Lawrence, I should like to sit with my daughter for a bit longer."

He nodded and exited the room, fighting the urge to run back to the bed, draw Selena close, and kiss her passionately.

CHAPTER TWELVE

The next morning

WHILE THEY HAD enjoyed a robust breakfast, Gerald found himself feeling anxious. He wanted—no, needed—to know more about what had taken place before Selena left home. What had driven her to ride to his manor home alone, through a rainstorm? Noticing that everyone seemed to have finished, he tapped his glass and stood.

"If we can adjourn to the drawing room, Selena has indicated she is ready to discuss it. She wants to hear everything that happened to her mother and I think what she has to say could be very important," he said, looking across the table at Selena.

She nodded. *I'm ready,* she mouthed.

"Darling, are you sure?"

"I am, Maman," she said. "I feel much better than yesterday."

He stepped behind Selena's chair and helped her stand, placing her hand on his arm. "Will everyone join us in the drawing room?"

A few minutes later, they were all settled in the drawing room.

"We are all here, Fleur. Selena can add her part of the story," Gerald's mother said.

"Lady Bowles, please take this seat next to Selena. After the journey you have been through, you need to be close to each other," Gerald said, seating himself next to his parents on the sofa. He had never been gladder to see them in his life. From the little Selena had muttered in her fevered ravings, despicable acts had taken place by Percival Bowles in her home.

Selena's mother began to speak, and her unbelievable story riveted everyone in the room.

"When the solicitor came to us and said they had found my husband's rightful heir, our initial reaction was relief," Lady Bowles said. "At least we could get on with our lives. But the man who met us was a monster. Having never met my husband's actual second cousin, Percival, we did not know someone might have been impersonating him. But I'm certain that no man of my husband's lineage could behave as this man did. Lord Percival Bowles arrived with a helper, a very large man he called Grom.

"Selena and I began to fear for our lives. Within two days of his arrival, Percival fired our loyal staff—except for Maggie, our cook, and her husband, the stable master, Ben—because their positions would have been harder to fill. All our dear staff, who were like family, were gone. We were alone, Selena and me—except for Maggie and Ben. They brought in women with loose morals from seedy taverns, and God only knows where the footmen came from. They all looked like they belonged in prison."

"How frightened you must have been," Gerald's mother murmured.

Lady Bowles nodded and gripped her hands together. "Percival demanded access to my husband's safe and that we turn over to him any funds we had in the house, including pin money that we might have saved. At first, he said, it was something he wanted to do to keep our things safe. But we suspected otherwise and tried to hide our things. However, Grom had already entered our rooms and taken what he could find. He didn't know what a few members of our most trusted staff knew…we maintained household money in hidden places, including my room and

Selena's. They were not large amounts, but enough should we need to leave at a moment's notice."

"That was very clever of you, my lady," Gerald said.

"It was something I learned from my own maman," she said softly. "Unfortunately, I had already told him of the betrothal when he first arrived. Before he showed us his true colors. But when I saw his furious reaction and the way he looked at my daughter, I realized immediately that something was wrong, and I withheld any information about Selena's inheritance, hoping that I had not put a target on her head.

"It did not take long for Percival to show us who he truly was. He would drink himself into a stupor each night, but not before engaging in lewd and despicable behavior with those women he'd hired. We could hear them at night. Selena and I stayed as far away as possible. We took to sleeping in the same room, locking the door, and lodging a chair under the doorknob.

"He kept us prisoners in our own home. We could not go anywhere and were barely allowed to speak to Maggie and Ben.

"Within two weeks of his arrival, I had become so sick I couldn't hold my head up. I told Selena she must leave and go to Lord Bellecote in London, or you, Lord Lawrence. She had received your invitation and planned to come here over Christmastide. But things had gotten so beyond our control that I feared for her life and made her promise me she would leave. I'm rarely ever ill, but I could barely hold my head up. We realized I was being poisoned—but Selena had not fallen ill, and so I was convinced he had plans for her. Horrible, evil plans. And we don't know what poison he used. I became so sick, my breathing was almost too shallow to detect.

"Cook summoned her husband, and somehow, they convinced the doctor what was happening. He pronounced me dead. Percival had them remove my body and prepare me for an immediate burial."

A collective gasp sounded from around the room.

"Oh, Maman," Selena sobbed.

"Instead, Maggie and Ben secreted me to Maggie's sister's home, and she and her sister Helen helped me recover. Ben weighted the coffin to feel like it held my body and nailed it shut so Percival would believe I was lying within. Percival had locked Selena in her room for most of the time I was ill, eliminating any possibility of reaching her. From what Ben found out, he told her I had succumbed to the fever but refused to let her attend my burial.

"On the day of my burial, Maggie and Ben had been able to drug the food and drink for everyone in the house—Percival was celebrating, guzzling my dear Phillip's whisky with a vengeance. The plan was to drug them and rescue Selena and bring her to Helen's home so that we could make our escape to London to your parents' townhouse. But when Maggie went to Selena's room, she could not find her. When Ben told her Azure was gone from the stables, they knew Selena must have escaped. They had no choice but to leave, and they collected me and we set off for London. I was still very ill but determined to go. We'd hoped to encounter Selena along the way, but we did not. I was beside myself with worry. But by the time we got to Bellecote House, his lordship and Lady Bellecote informed us about your missive, Lord Lawrence."

Gerald nodded.

"The missive had arrived less than an hour before we did. And they informed us that Selena had arrived here at Bellwood and that she'd had an accident and hurt her head, but that she was stable and resting under a doctor's care. I was worried but also relieved that my daughter was safe here with you."

"She's a very brave young lady," Gerald's father said.

"She is indeed," Gerald replied, scarcely able to contain his fury at what Selena and her mother had endured.

"Asher arrived that same evening," his father added. "He told us you'd sent him a missive as well. And we made plans to come here as soon as possible. But there is something more to this story that you do not know."

Gerald raised a questioning brow at his father.

"I know Percival Bowles very well. He's a friend of many years. That man at Rose Manor is not Percival Bowles. He's an imposter."

"How do you know?" Gerald asked.

"Because I told him."

Gerald looked up to see his friend Wright in the doorway of the dining room.

"Wright!" He stood to greet his friend and invited him to join them.

"My apologies—I only just arrived," Wright said.

"Tell Gerald what you know," Banbury said.

Wright nodded. "As soon as I got your missive, Gerald, I went to Bellecote House. Lady Bowles was exhausted and resting when I arrived, but I questioned Maggie and Ben. They described Percival and his minion Grom. I knew immediately who they were—Vern Stiles and Grom Dugan. Vern has a tattoo of some sort of dragon on one side of his neck."

"Yes, there was some sort of drawing on his neck. But part of it was always covered in my presence," Lady Bowles said.

"And there is an identifying mark on the real Lord Percival Bowles…a tattoo of an anchor, with the year 1808 below it on the inside of his right wrist. It's not overly large, but it signifies the year he started in the Merchant Service," Wright added.

"Then what happened to him?" Gerald asked.

"We are trying to determine that," his father said. "He was reported missing from his post with the Merchant Service, but that is all we know."

"Percival had become a peer, and if he met with foul play, the prince regent wants to know. Before we left, Prinny ordered that men be dispatched to investigate and determine if the real Percival is alive or dead," Banbury said. "Lord Wright has been looking into the new Viscount Bowles's background. He has many connections in the Merchant Service, as well as the regular navy. He may know more."

They turned and looked at Wright. He nodded. "I've known Percival for years, and none of this sounds like him. However, I'm not defending him. We don't know what has happened—yet—to Percival, but we suspect foul play."

"There has to have been *some* sort of foul play," Gerald's father agreed. "My friend died thinking he had left his wife and daughter in safety."

"He ordered me to pack my valise for Gretna Green and told me we would leave the next day," Selena said. "He said Maman had already been buried. I packed my valise with what money I still had in my secret place in the floorboards, and the only jewels I still had...a few things Maman and Papa had given to me, including my sapphire ring, Grand-mere's pearls, and Papa's signet ring. I thought I would need to sell them to survive. I found apples and carrots for Azure and wore the clothes that I usually rode when I rode him, britches and a shirt. We ran into much rain, and I would not have been able to travel to London in such weather. Both Azure and I were almost to the point of exhaustion. I decided to come here, as it was closer than London. And I didn't think Percival could find me here. If he did, I felt certain you would protect me, Gerald."

Gerald swallowed. She had trusted him with her life. "I will continue to protect you, Selena," he said, unable to control the misting in his eyes as he gazed at her. "Do you remember what happened in the stables that led to your fainting?" He swallowed, pushing past the lump in his throat. *I thought I had lost you...just when I found you, Selena.*

"Yes," Selena replied softly.

"Well, now that your memory has returned, do you still feel the same way about our betrothal?" he asked in a raspy voice.

"Yes, I do."

He drew her close and held her, planting a kiss on her cheek.

When he let her go, Gerald said, "I'm not sure everyone was privy to what happened when Selena arrived, so if you'd like, I can fill you in on it."

There was a general murmuring of agreement.

"Dutch was outside, walking the property and making sure the fences were intact, when the rain began to fall. It had become customary for me to do it in the evenings. I made it into the shelter, but Dutch had run ahead. Thinking he was in the stables, I heard him give a warning bark outside, from behind the barn. I ran out and saw him cornering a large gray stallion with what I thought was a small boy riding him. The stallion reared up and threw you from his back. Your head hit a large rock when you landed, and when you awoke the next morning, you had no memory. Not until yesterday afternoon, during our walk in the stables. Something caused you extreme head pain, and you fainted."

Dutch barked, and everyone laughed, all needing a moment of relief. Gerald had forgotten the dog had followed them in here, but he had always allowed Dutch to go where he wanted inside the house or out. "He knows we are talking about him."

Banbury spoke up. "Selena, you spent a considerable amount of time around the supposed viscount. Selena, do either you or your mother recall seeing a tattoo on his wrist?"

Lady Bowles shook her head and looked at her daughter.

CHAPTER THIRTEEN

S ELENA COULDN'T SHAKE her last memory of Lord Percival
Bowles. Her heart pounded in her throat as she remembered
his visit to her room the night he'd told her, almost gleefully, that
her mother had died. He had attacked her, taunting her and
insisting she would marry him. The lecherous man had grabbed
her and pushed her against the wall, his stale whisky breath nearly
smothering her as he forced his vile mouth on hers, while his
coal-black eyes bored into her own. As much as she wanted not to
recall the horrible attack, she closed her eyes and saw it all, every
last disgusting detail, as he abused her and mocked her with
acerbic laughter. He had adjusted his sleeves after he let her go
and told her to pack for Gretna Green, before leaving her room.

She would never forget the sight and feel of those repulsive
hands and that revolting mouth. But in a flash of memory, there
was something else she saw…

"I remember… I remember seeing his right wrist. It was
when he adjusted his right sleeve. There was no tattoo. I would
have remembered that after what he did," she said, looking away.

"What did he do, Selena?" Gerald asked. His voice had a
steely calmness to it.

"H-he hurt me…" she stammered. "But not in the way you
might think. I mean, he didn't…" Selena swallowed, unable to
finish the sentence. How could she possibly tell this room full of

people that the man had assaulted her…and then bitten her? She couldn't. Shame consumed her. *What must Gerald and his family think of me—the woman he's betrothed to marry?*

"Did he hit you?" Wright asked.

She nodded, and her eyes filled with tears. "He was brutal." She noticed that Gerald's face flushed a deep shade of red, and the tightness of his jaw conveyed his mounting anger.

"Miss Bowles, your information revealed valuable information about the man, and we appreciate the effort it took to relive it," Wright said.

"Thank you, Lord Wright," Selena said.

"Rest assured we will stop him and mete out justice," Gerald said with a steely voice.

She took her mother's hand and squeezed it. Percival was a despicable demon, and he had soiled her. How could Gerald possibly want to marry a woman who had been defiled? She bit her bottom lip, worried that Percival had done more—perhaps something she hadn't recalled yet.

She needed to tell Gerald everything she remembered. They had made a pact to keep no more secrets, but she was filled with fear and uncertainty about how he would react. She couldn't delay the conversation forever, but the thought of losing him made her heart thunder in panic.

"I'm feeling tired. If you will excuse me, I'd like to lie down for a little while," Selena said. It was true, she was exhausted, but she was also stalling. She needed to gather her thoughts before facing Gerald with the ugly truth.

"Allow me to walk you upstairs, Selena," he said, helping her to her feet.

Selena nodded, and as she leaned on him for support, she sensed his eagerness to talk things through, but she couldn't bring herself to do it. Despite her inner conflict, she found comfort in his touch and his nearness and longed for his reassurance.

"I need to ask for your forgiveness," Gerald said as they reached the third-floor landing.

"Forgive *you*? But why?" she asked, confused at his request. She was the one who was keeping secrets. Gerald had admitted everything to her.

"I feel like the worst cad. The thought of that filthy man touching you made my blood boil, and I wanted to tear the man from limb to limb. But I shouldn't have pressed you—especially not in front of everyone. I am sorry, Selena, truly. Can you forgive me?"

"Of course, Gerald. You have questions and you have a right to ask those questions of me. We are betrothed. I just need some time. It's like all these feelings and memories have flooded into my head. And I'm still trying to sort through them. I never imagined that regaining my memory would be so fatiguing."

"Perhaps we can take a walk this afternoon when after you've had a chance to rest."

"I should like that very much," she replied with a smile.

He drew her close and tilted her face up to his. "Nothing that you could say could change anything about how I feel about you. My desire to make you my wife remains unwavering," he whispered. Leaning down, he kissed her passionately, conveying his deep affection and commitment.

She eagerly ran her fingers through his hair, drawing him even closer, adrift in his familiar scent of sandalwood, citrus, and leather. Lost in the moment, she wanted the kiss to continue when he stepped back. "Thank you, Gerald." She relished the warmth of his arms around her.

He opened the door of her bedchamber and lifted her hand to his lips. "Until later."

"Until later," she echoed softly. A nap would do her a world of good, and hopefully, she would be able to gather her strength to tell him the truth.

"Then I shall see you in a few hours, love," he said with a tender smile, before bending down and placing a gentle kiss on her forehead.

AS HE MADE his way to this study, Gerald thought about the revelations that Selena and her mother had shared. The torturous existence they had endured was ghastly to think about. Selena had been led to believe her mother had died. Thank God for Ben and Maggie and their efforts. It was the only reason Selena still had her mother. He would find a suitable way to thank them.

Entering his study, he saw his father, brother-in-law, and best friend engaged in a vigorous discussion about the Percival Bowles imposter.

"Have you determined where that bastard is hiding?" Gerald asked, closing the door behind him.

"We don't know, but we plan to find him," Wright said. "After hearing Lady Bowles's account, it was wise that you all left when you did. The man will be looking for Miss Bowles. She thwarted him once, and men like Vern Stiles don't take kindly to being denied what they want. My guess is London would be one of the first places he'll look."

"Our home has been staffed with extra footmen and it's being watched," Gerald's father said. "And so is Lady Bowles's townhouse. As soon as he's spotted, the men have been instructed to send word."

"Connery helped me house extra security here and in a few empty buildings throughout the estate," Wright said.

"I appreciate that," Gerald said. "I'm sure Stiles will come here after he realizes his prey is not in London. How quickly do you think he will learn of this location?"

"I don't think it will take too long to locate Bellwood," Banbury said. "Your rendezvous at the Adamsons' ball five years ago was a topic of gossip for months. Everyone knew you moved to your father's recently purchased estate. That was no secret."

"Even so, it would take days for the bastard to ride to London, then a similar amount of time to come here," Gerald's father said.

"When he does, we'll be ready for him," Gerald said.

"We will, son." His father reached out and patted his shoulder.

"And we're fortunate that Prinny is determined to find the imposter before he tries to flee," Wright said. "He was incensed this could happen to one of his peers and sent men to Portugal, the last port the real Percival was known to have visited. He also sent men to Lady Bowles's estate. Based on what we've surmised, the real Percival Bowles disappeared shortly after getting off his ship several weeks ago. Miss Bowles's account confirms what we've suspected. When he is caught, Vern Stiles and his accomplice will know no peace for the rest of what will be their short lives."

Gerald's face heated with anger. "When I get my hands on him, he'll regret ever touching her," he said, accepting a glass of brandy from his father. He took a large gulp. "I have a bad feeling about all of this. I don't want to just sit around speculating. We've got to do something, now."

The four men spent the next hour talking about what they knew and fielding different scenarios.

"Stay close to Selena, son," his father warned. "What she has been through is more than any woman should have to endure. And should this blackguard slip through our net, he will come straight for her. Keep in mind, too, that he thinks Lady Bowles is deceased."

"I will, Father. I promise." He meant it. There was no way he would abandon Selena. She was the bravest woman that he knew, and the thought that she was still willing to marry him after all he had done to destroy their betrothal still astonished him. The imposter would regret laying a hand on her.

Banbury stood up and stretched. "Friends, I need to check on Diana and the babies. We will remain vigilant here."

"Thank you, Banbury," Gerald said, giving his brother-in-law a hearty slap on the back.

"I should check on the men," Wright said after downing the rest of his brandy. "Connery has several housed in the stables, in the rooms you built in the back, and in any other spare housing throughout the estate. We want to make sure we've got the manor covered from every angle—day and night. By the way, my compliments to you and Connery. This property is extraordinary. You've restored it beyond my imagination."

"Thanks, friend," Gerald said, shaking his hand.

"I too am greatly impressed by what you've done here, son," his father said after Banbury and Wright left.

"This is the first time you've been here," Gerald said. "It took a while, but I feel good about what we've accomplished here."

"How is your relationship with the local villagers and the tenant farmers in the area?"

"They've been very helpful, and we've been helpful in return. We've built a good rapport with the locals. It took time to gain their trust, but I made it one of my goals to help improve the lives of everyone in the area. So far, I've been able to pay for new roofs for all the tenant farmers' homes. And in return, they helped with the refurbishment of the manor house, and in particular the stonework, including the stone wall. We've also started working on the grounds and found our new gardener from within the community. He is the brother of one of our tenants. He has a true skill in planting and crop rotation."

"All sound ideas," his father said.

Gerald blew out a breath. "Unfortunately, since Selena's arrival, I've fallen behind getting the house ready for the festivities. However, Mrs. Evans and Mrs. McDonald are planning baskets for each of the families. Dr. Baker has been a great resource—making sure we know those in need of additional help."

"That's good to hear. Your mother will be pleased. As for decorating the manor, we have an entire house full of intelligent and creative ladies who will no doubt step in and organize everything in a matter of days."

They both chuckled.

"I noticed that you and Selena have grown very close," his father said after a pause. "Five years ago, you'd have given everything to be free of this betrothal."

Gerald felt his face flush. "Yes, I know. And I was wrong, Father. My behavior was abominable. I deliberately did things to sabotage the betrothal and embarrass the family. For that, I am truly sorry. Getting to know Selena… Well, she's unlike any woman I've ever met. The betrothal I once hated has turned out to be the best thing that has ever happened to me."

His father smiled. "I can see you mean that."

"I've changed, Father."

"No, son, you haven't changed. You've become the man I always knew was inside you. I'm proud of you." He reached out to squeeze Gerald's shoulder.

"Thank you, Father. Your praise means a great deal to me," Gerald said, swallowing the lump in his throat.

Chapter Fourteen

Later that afternoon

"Mrs. McDonald, those apple tarts you served for lunch were delicious," Fleur said.

"Oh, thank you so much, milady. It's a favorite around here," the cook said. "I enjoy making them."

"I hope you don't mind my popping into the kitchen, but I'd like to visit my daughter's horse. Would you have a couple of apples to spare?" Fleur hadn't seen the horse in weeks and needed to see him and thank him for bringing her daughter safely to Lord Lawrence's estate.

A shiver coursed down her back as she realized how close she had been to losing her daughter. If not for that horse—who had surely been an angel in disguise—she might have lost her dear Selena. She could not even imagine having survived her near death from poisoning only to discover her precious daughter had either gone missing or been killed. God forbid. She did not know if she could have gone on if something had happened to Selena.

"Of course, Lady Bowles." Cook dried her hands on her apron. "I have a small basket you can use to carry them. Those horses love 'em."

"Is someone going to the stables?" Connery asked as he walked into the kitchen.

"Yes, Mr. Connery. I thought I'd check on my daughter's horse," Fleur said, stepping forward and giving him a tentative smile.

"I'm heading that way as well. May I accompany you?" Connery asked.

"I would appreciate that, Mr. Connery."

He rubbed the back of his neck and looked around distractedly. "Ah, Mrs. McDonald, have I missed out again? Are they gone?"

The plump little cook gave a wide smile and pulled a towel off a bowl. "I took a plate of them into the study for his lordship's meeting, but I saved you two." She handed him two tarts wrapped in a kitchen towel.

"Ah, Mrs. McDonald, you are the best." Connery grinned, leaning down and bussing the older woman on the cheek. He tucked the apple tarts in his pocket, giving it a little pat.

Fleur couldn't help but smile at the gleeful look on the man's face. To see such a tall and rugged man smiling like a boy over apple tarts made her heart all aflutter. A feeling she hadn't experienced since she was a young debutante at her first ball.

Angus Connery was certainly a most impressive man, almost as tall as Lord Lawrence and every bit as muscular, no doubt from a lifetime of managing estates.

He turned to her and smiled, making her forget herself. "My lady, there is a chill in the air, so you may want to wear your pelisse."

She'd started to go back for her wrap when Anna walked in carrying it. "There ye are, Lady Bowles. I overheard you tell Mr. Wells that you'd be at the stables and saw your pelisse still hanging on the coat stand. So I thought I'd bring it to ye."

"Anna, you're a fine lass. Thank you for thinking of that." Connery held the cloak for Fleur as she slipped it on.

"Miss Selena is still sleeping?" Fleur asked the young maid.

"Yes, milady. Sleeping peacefully, last I checked on her."

Fleur heaved a deep sigh. "I am glad to hear it."

"I'll keep watch over her while you're on your walk."

"Thank you, my dear," Fleur said, giving Anna's hand a gentle squeeze.

The young maid curtseyed and left.

"Shall we go, milady?" Connery asked.

"Yes, please. I thought this would be a good opportunity to spend time with Azure and thank him for keeping my daughter safe," Fleur said.

Connery chuckled. "I don't doubt he would understand you." He accepted the basket of apples from Mrs. McDonald and he and Fleur left the house together through the kitchen door. "What a fine specimen of horseflesh that one is. Where did you find him?"

"It's a remarkable story, really," Fleur said.

"I've admired that horse since he arrived and would love to hear it."

"Very well," she said, smiling. "My husband Phillip was returning home from London—this was a few years before his passing." Despite the health complications he suffered in later life, he had been a very good husband and father. She missed him. "Phillip heard a loud gunshot and then someone shouting for help. He described seeing an out-of-control rig with an older gentleman trying desperately to regain control of the horses. But the man was having little luck, and Phillip urged his own mount forward. He overtook the rig and—*somehow*—managed to move from his own horse to the rig and stop it.

"Phillip stood tall and proud, much like you," she said, feeling the heat creeping up her neck. She dared a peek at Connery and saw his lips twitch. Eager to shift the focus away from her own embarrassment, she continued speaking as they strolled along. "He was a man who had always prided himself on his horsemanship, despite his slowly declining health. He managed to grab hold of the reins of the horses, saving the stranger from grievous injury. After they introduced themselves and exchanged a few friendly words about the spirit of horses, Phillip bade him a courteous farewell.

"A year passed, and a man appeared at Rose Point looking for my husband. He said the older man had died and left specific instructions to gift a special horse to Phillip. The man was adamant that this horse was for my husband to do with as he wanted to. Azure was a year old at the time and had the most remarkable eyes...almost the same color as Selena's. Our daughter has always loved horses and shared her father's equine talents. Phillip gifted the horse to our daughter...and I will say it was love at first sight. I do not doubt that Azure would have given his life to protect her. That's how close they are." She blinked back tears as she remembered that first touching meeting.

From the corner of her eye, she could see Connery looking at her, and the expression in his eyes made her breath catch. If she wasn't careful, she could easily lose her heart to this man... But oh, how she'd missed being looked at that way by a man. Not since those early years with Phillip, before life and his health began to take precedence.

"That's a remarkable story. And from what I recall, I think you are right," Connery said.

"Yes. When we were home, there wasn't a day that Selena didn't visit that horse, and she rode him every chance she got. The man's note to my husband had specified the thoroughbred lineage, but I don't recall the specifics. They may be in my husband's papers at Rose Point."

"We knew he was thoroughbred, and a valuable one at that. Your daughter arrived in the middle of a rainstorm. I'm certain you've heard the story from Gerald—Lord Lawrence."

"Yes, I did. I know that Azure would never have reacted that way had he not been spooked and under such extreme circum-stances."

"Selena visited him after she came through her fever, and it was that visit that triggered her memory to come back," Connery said. "I can see they have a unique relationship. Your daughter is a very special young lady with a truly remarkable gift in being able to communicate with horses."

"She's always had that gift. From when she was a little girl,"

Fleur said.

"I can see where she gets her beauty and her strength from," he said softly.

"I thank you, Mr. Connery," Fleur said, feeling that heat of a blush yet again.

"I would be honored if you would call me Angus," he said.

"Thank you, Angus. Please call me Fleur."

"Fleur," he said in a voice that was both gruff and sensual. "Flower. A lovely name for a lovely woman."

Feeling another blush heating her cheeks, she thanked him again, and they continued on their walk to the stables.

Angus led her through the stables, pointing out the horses. As they approached Azure's stall, a stable boy was hanging up the horse's brush.

"Look how this horse gleams, Mr. Connery. His coat starts gray, but after you brush him, he looks more silver. And those eyes...I've never seen the like," the stable boy declared.

"Aye, you did a fine job brushing him, Joshua," Angus said, patting the boy on the shoulder. The lad beamed at Angus.

Fleur extracted an apple from her skirt and held it toward Azure. The horse whinnied and nodded.

"A real beauty," Angus said.

Fleur glanced at him, but he wasn't looking at the horse. Not used to such overt admiration, she turned her gaze to Azure.

"Did your daughter train the horse?" Angus asked.

"She did. She has been helping my husband and his stable master with horses since she learned to ride."

"Mr. Connery, I almost forgot," Joshua said. "You asked me to let you know when Lady Bowles's stable master and his wife arrived. They just arrived only a few minutes ago. Mr. Ghent and his wife are still with their rig. He insisted that he would take care of the horses. I've given them two stalls on the back row for their mares and set out the water for them. I offered to feed them, but he wants to do it."

"That's just like Ben," Fleur said. "He's always taken such

good care of our horses."

"I am thankful they helped you survive that blackguard's poisonous attack," Angus said.

"Yes. I was weaker than a newborn babe. Maggie took care of me, hand-feeding me broth and gruel until I could hold my head up."

A shiver overtook her as she recalled the first time she felt well enough to hold any part of a conversation. She had nearly died at the hands of Vern Stiles. "Thank God for Maggie and Ben."

"I would like to welcome them," Angus said. "Would you care to come with me?"

She looked at the horse, who was munching on his third apple. "Thank you, Azure—thank you for taking care of my girl." The horse bobbed his head, seeming to understand. She reached up and gently pulled his nose to her. "Thank you," she said, kissing him on his nose.

Azure whinnied his approval.

She heard their voices before she saw them and rushed in their direction. "Maggie! Ben! I'm so happy to see you both," Fleur said, throwing her arms around the couple and hugging them. "This is Mr. Angus Connery, the estate manager for Bellwood. He has been working with Lord Lawrence on this gorgeous estate."

Angus warmly greeted both Ben and Maggie, welcoming them to Bellwood.

Ben blew out a whistle. "'Tis one of the most beautiful estates I've seen—excepting Rose Point, of course. At least to my eye. If the grounds along the main road and the stables are any indication of what to expect in the main house, Mr. Connery and Lord Lawrence have outdone themselves."

"Thank you, Ben. I would like to take credit, but most of it belongs to Lord Lawrence, as he worked on the grounds. And truthfully, he turned a dead estate into a profitable one," Angus said. He smiled at the Ghents. "What you both did took courage.

We wouldn't have Lady Bowles with us today if not for that courage. We appreciate you both so much."

"We did what was right, Mr. Connery. We have worked for the Bowles family for many years. We consider them our people—our family. And that man…" Ben choked up. "He nearly killed her, he did."

Touched at the raw emotion displayed by Ben, Fleur swallowed past the lump in her throat. "As we, too, have always considered you both family," she said, dabbing at the corners of her watery eyes.

"Let's get you settled," Angus said. "Ben, you and your lovely missus may enter the house from any door you'd like. But the kitchen is the closest." He turned and gave them directions to the door leading into the kitchen. "Your room is ready, and you will probably find Mrs. Evans, the housekeeper, in her office, which is a small room in the hall just off the kitchen. And you will also meet Mrs. McDonald, our cook. She will want to make sure you have a hot meal."

"Thank you, sir," Ben replied. "It's been a while since we've eaten today, and that sounds most inviting. We appreciate you letting us stay here."

"Nonsense. We would not have it any other way, but you must promise to let me know if you need anything," Angus said.

"Selena has been fatigued of late and sleeping much of the day. But she will be thrilled to see you both in the morning," Fleur said.

"Oh? She's not ill, is she, milady?" Maggie asked.

"She was injured but is much improved," Fleur said. She hoped her daughter would be up and about more tomorrow. She had observed the budding relationship between her daughter and Lord Lawrence but wondered if problems had emerged between the two.

"I'm looking forward to seeing the child—please let her know we will do anything we can to help her back to her old self," Maggie said.

"I will, my dear Maggie." Fleur wrapped the older woman in a warm embrace.

"I'm ready to eat and turn in, if you are, wife," Ben said, stifling a yawn. He held out his arm. His wife nodded and took it.

Angus and Fleur watched the couple stroll to the manor.

"It's easy to see the affection they have for you and Selena," Angus said.

"It's mutual."

"You and your daughter are courageous women."

Fleur gave a slight shake of her head. "Thank you. That is generous of you to say. What Selena did was brave. But not me… I am not brave. Had I been brave, I would have slit that *cochon*'s neck while he slept!"

Connery threw back his head and laughed. For a moment, they stared at each other.

Something shifted inside Fleur. "Would you…that is…would you like to walk with me for a while?" The fresh air and the lovely surroundings called to her.

"I would enjoy walking with you," he said in that gruff-soft voice. "Allow me to show you this splendid estate," he offered, holding out his arm.

He was looking at her with that gleam again. Fleur couldn't help but be flattered and a little flustered by his attention.

She hadn't found herself attracted to another man since before Phillip. Theirs had been an arranged marriage, but they grew to love each other. However, Phillip had been more than twenty years older, and not in the best of health. While she had grieved his passing deeply and missed his humor, wisdom, and loving heart, she had long since accepted that she would never grow old with him. Her recent horrid experience with that fiendish imposter was something she had never expected. And her own brush with death at the hand of that demon had left her shaken and vulnerable. She had thought herself a strong and capable woman, but she had not been able to cope and almost lost her life in the process—and the life of her beloved daughter as well.

Thank God for Selena's courage and presence of mind to ride to Gerald's estate. Fleur prayed that their betrothal would flourish into a loving relationship. And from what she'd observed of the two of them together, their feelings were very strongly engaged.

As they took a shortcut through a field on the way to a road below them, she blew out a shallow breath she didn't realize she had been holding. She had never taken too much notice of other men while Phillip lived, but this man beside her was undeniably attractive. With his thick silver hair mixed with dark brown, a strong, dimpled chin, and dark blue eyes, she found it increasingly hard to take her attention away from him. A small smile formed on her lips as she recalled his deep, throaty laugh. His laugh had her toes curling, and she hadn't felt her toes curl in years. Briefly, she wondered what it might be like to kiss him.

They approached a small pond surrounded by apple trees, and he led her to a small stone bench, where they sat.

"What a lovely spot. This property seems to have plenty of water," Fleur commented, surveying the area around the pond. "Are there fish?"

"Aye. Occasionally, I take advantage of the stock and fish for our dinner. And you're right. 'Tis a lovely property. I enjoy living here."

"Wh-what about your life?" Fleur asked. "Where did you live before you arrived here? Did you never marry?"

"AYE. SHE WAS a bonnie lass. She died giving birth to my son. My son died with her." Angus realized he hadn't spoken of Beatrice in a very long time.

"I'm so sorry."

"Ach! It feels like a lifetime ago. Ten years. The pain isn't as raw as it once was." He had loved Beatrice with all his heart, and the grief he'd felt at losing her and the babe had been devastating, but he'd learned to live with that loss—and over time, life had become bearable. "I'm sure you ken my meaning. You lost your husband only a year ago. I am sorry for your loss." He stole a glance at the beautiful woman beside him. Her soft brown curls framed her face, and with her deep blue eyes, he found her very pleasing. Aye, time had healed his soul, but he did miss the love of a good woman. He wasn't the type to keep a mistress or indulge in fleeting liaisons. He wanted a woman who shared his interests.

"I do. And I confess this last year has been a hard time of adjustments, not to mention a murdering imposter claiming Rose Point as his," she said.

"Knowing Gerald and Wright and Banbury, that willna be for much longer," he said.

"Lord Lawrence has certainly impressed me. He is much changed from the brash and bold rapscallion he once was."

"Aye, well, young men need to sow a few wild oats before they become who they are truly meant to be."

"When Lord Lawrence's mother wrote to me five years ago after that unfortunate incident at the Adamsons' ball, telling me that her son had been sent to this estate without a farthing, I did not fully believe it. It seemed inconceivable that an earl would do that to his heir."

Angus chuckled. "He did indeed do that. And I fully support-ed it. But it did not take Gerald long to take the reins of his life and his future. My admiration for the lad took root. He was a determined young man and he accomplished every goal he set out to achieve, including developing an interest in thorough-breds."

"I agree, he has changed," she said. "He has carried his re-sponsibilities well. I can see he has taken care of my daughter as though they were already married."

"Lord Lawrence is a good man—and most determined," Connery said. "It was a good thing, because he did not have the luxuries he was used to back in London or at the family estate—

no valet, and a very small household staff."

"Something tells me there is a story there," Fleur said with a smile.

"When we got here, the stables didn't exist because it had burned down shortly after the previous owner abandoned the property. As a result, there were stray animals everywhere—those that hadn't already been claimed or taken by local villagers or tenant farmers. Gerald rounded up a pig and asked me what to do with it. Earlier in the week, I had identified an old pigpen and repaired it—and I watered it. When he finally wrestled the pig into the pen, I happened by. The poor man was covered to his ears in mud. I tell you, the lad kept slipping and sliding. He finally used the pig to help himself up. When he saw me watching, I thought he was going to lose his temper, but he didn't. He burst into laughter and told me he couldn't wait to have roast pig."

"Perhaps the pig was integral to helping him become the good man he is today." Fleur laughed.

At her tinkling laugh, he turned and gazed at her warmly. "Your laugh is so sweet… It reminds me of a beautiful place we called Crystal Brook back home. It was named for its tinkling sound. So lovely."

Fleur blushed at the compliment. And he couldn't help but think how youthful and pretty she was. "Goodness! They say that French men have silver tongues, but I think it is the Scottish, no?"

Angus laughed.

Under the darkening sky, Angus and Fleur resumed their stroll around the pond and over the lush grounds surrounding the estate. As they continued to exchange playful banter, the distant rumble of thunder reverberated through the air, heralding an approaching storm.

"Where did that come from?" Fleur asked.

"The weather's quick shifts in this area have never failed to amaze me," Angus said.

Worried that Fleur might catch a cold—or worse, given her recent illness—he removed his jacket and held it above their heads to shield them from the large drops of rain that had begun to fall. "Let's hurry before it turns into a deluge," he said.

He was actually thankful for the rain, for it gave him an excuse to wrap a protective arm around Fleur's delicate shoulders as they hurried back to the manor. He was no fool, nor a wee lad at his first ceilidh. He knew when a woman was attracted to him. But he was not looking for a mere flirtation. Not with a woman like Fleur. He'd never met a woman like her, and the need to protect her was strong, as was his admiration for her strength. He hoped that Gerald and Wright caught the bastard who'd done this to Fleur and Selena soon so that both women could resume their lives without the fear of being attacked again.

CHAPTER FIFTEEN

The next day

GERALD RETURNED FROM his morning ride, still shrouded by the morning fog. He had toured the grounds closest to the manor house and was satisfied with the security detail that surrounded and protected the estate, including the large number of footmen Wright had hired positioned with rifles around the grounds.

Gerald slid down from Aphrodite and walked the thoroughbred into the stables, his anger still burning over what he'd learned about the imposter who'd hurt Selena and her mother. The fact that Selena had been accosted in such a vile manner and narrowly escaped a brutal rape erupted a fire of fury inside him. When they tracked down the bastard posing as Lord Percival, Gerald would rip off his limbs and enjoy doing it.

Yesterday, following her emotional description of the last time she'd seen the man calling himself Lord Percival, Selena's energy seemed to evaporate. He'd planned to speak to her on their walk, hoping to hear more of what had happened. He needed to hear the full story. But her need to sleep quashed his hope to take a walk. When she lay down for a short nap, she ended up sleeping straight through the day and night.

Resigned to waiting, Gerald led Aphrodite into her stall. Startled when he heard Selena's soft voice at the other end of the stable, he handed Aphrodite's reins to Joshua, who had been delivering fresh hay to the stall. "I'll take good care of her, your lordship."

"Thank you, Joshua. She had a long ride and needs to be brushed."

Approaching Selena, he slowed to listen.

"Azure, it's so good to see you, my sweet boy. I brought you an apple and some carrots," she whispered. "But don't tell anyone."

Gerald grinned as Azure gave a soft snort in reply.

"I'm so lucky to have you, Azure," she murmured. As the horse munched, she gently patted his neck.

"Good morning," Gerald said.

Selena turned in surprise, her hand going to her chest.

"Forgive me, I didn't mean to startle you."

A glowing smile lit her face and his breath hitched at the beauty of it.

"Oh! Good morning, Gerald. You did not startle me—I was just sneaking Azure some treats." She winked, and Gerald's heart did a dozen somersaults.

He looked at the dark-haired woman standing next to him. She was brave and beautiful, and when she was near, he struggled to control the feelings that stirred within him. "Selena, could we take a walk? Do you feel up to it?"

Pleasure lit up the beautiful blue eyes that regarded him. She nodded. After handing Azure another carrot, she kissed her horse on the nose. Smiling up at Gerald, she said, "I'd like that very much."

As THEY WALKED away from the stables, she felt Gerald's hand grip hers and squeeze. She knew he was trying to reassure her, but he didn't know everything. He didn't know everything because she hadn't told him. And she'd promised she wouldn't keep secrets. But this one hurt so much, she didn't know how to tell him—but tell him she must.

Selena wished she had never recalled the memory of that night with Percival. The vile man had molested her. She felt nothing but the heat of shame.

"I apologize for sleeping so long yesterday."

"Selena, you slept almost a full day. You obviously needed it, love. I've just missed you."

He probably won't miss me when he hears everything, she thought. One day he'd be an earl—how could he possibly want a wife who was sullied? "I was tired. I don't think I've ever been that tired, Gerald."

"I never meant to add to your anxiety, love. I shouldn't have pressed you to give more details...not in front of my family."

"You did nothing wrong. Your request was reasonable." She *needed* to tell him. They had promised no more secrets. "It's just that...the return of my memory has taken me by surprise as well. I have remembered things, you see, things I wish I could forget, but I cannot."

"Sometimes sharing those difficult and painful memories can help," Gerald suggested in a soft voice.

She glanced at him, and he was looking at her with such concern that all she wanted to do was feel his arms around her tight and breathe in his strength.

"Remember when I was feverish and kissed you."

"Yes, I recall you were quite brazen," he said, his voice deep and teasing.

"And then the day of our wonderful picnic when you kissed me."

"Alas, I could not help myself. You were just so irresistible." He leaned down to whisper in her ear. "I'd be happy to oblige again."

She felt the heat of a blush as she glanced at him; his smile was teasing but his eyes held an intensity that made her chest constrict. "Oh, well, my…" She stumbled, not knowing what to say.

He chuckled and wrapped his arm around her, drawing her close. He dropped a kiss on top of her head. "It's all right, my sweet—I would never do anything that would make you uncomfortable. I promise," he added softly.

She nodded and blinked back sudden tears. "You have been so kind and patient. But I need to tell you something…"

He stopped walking and turned her to face him. His eyes were now serious, looking at her with concern. "You want to tell me about that man, the imposter who pretended to be Percival Bowles."

"Yes. But, you see, I have to tell you that when we kissed, it wasn't my first kiss. I thought it was, but then when my memory returned, I realized that it wasn't, because…because…that m-man…that horrible man assaulted m-me. He pushed me up against the w-wall and held my hands above my head, and his lips… It wasn't a kiss…but it was like he attacked me with his mouth and he g-groped me…" A sob escaped her, and she covered her mouth and turned her head away from Gerald.

She felt Gerald's strong arms go around her, and she turned into his chest and cried, "N-no matter how much I f-fought, I wasn't strong enough to stop him from t-touching me with those vile hands and his teeth. I remember breath, stale and vile, the stench nearly choking me. And his h-hands were like claws… But I h-have to tell you. He didn't… He didn't do…"

"Hush, my love," Gerald whispered, kissing her forehead. "I know. I know."

Tears streamed from her eyes. "I'm so s-sorry, Gerald. You m-must think me wanton. And I will release you f-from any obligation. My father wouldn't have expected you to honor a betrothal to a soiled woman."

"Selena, what are you talking about?" He held her face and looked down at her, his eyes wide with shock. "Why would you say that?"

"Because I am not who you thought I was. I'd give anything to reclaim the bliss of believing that you were the first man to kiss me, but I can't unremember what happened."

"My love, you did nothing wrong. What happened to you was a violation. That bastard attacked you. That was not a kiss he gave you. He forced himself upon you, and I thank God that you did not suffer any more than you did. But what you went through was not your fault. And I am only sorry that you had to go through it alone. But the fact that you escaped and rode all the way here—in a rainstorm, no less—only shows how courageous and strong you are."

"You think I'm brave and strong?"

"Yes. Yes. I do!"

"So, you forgive me for what happened?"

"Oh, Selena." He held her tight and kissed her forehead again. "There is nothing to forgive."

"But—I'm not the woman you thought I was."

"Do you remember forgiving me the day of the picnic when I admitted to you about that stupid bet, the one I made at the Adamsons' ball five years ago?"

"Yes."

"Even though you had amnesia at the time, you said that no matter what, even if and when your memory returned, you would still feel the same way. That you forgave me...and now that you remember what you saw me do that night five years ago, how do you feel? Do you still forgive me?"

"Yes, of course, without question."

"Do you hold it against me?"

"No. I would never do that."

"Then why would you think that I would reject you after finding out what that vile man did to you?" he asked. "Selena, I'm angry at that bastard for what he did to you, tried to do to you and your mother, and for what he still wants to do to you. And I'm so sorry I was a cad to you five years ago. You didn't deserve that, and you don't deserve any of this pain. Knowing how strong and courageous and wonderful you are, how incredible and clever and kind—how could I do anything but fall in love with you? I love you, Selena. I love you. I love you so very much."

"Y-you love me?" She looked up into his sable eyes, and the warmth and love she saw in his gaze nearly took her breath away.

"I do. I think I've loved you since the night of the storm as I carried you up the stairs. You were covered in mud and dirt, and for a moment you opened those incredible blue eyes and said, 'Lord Lawrence. I found you,' and everything changed," he said. "I looked into the most beautiful blue eyes that I have ever seen and knew who you were. Your courage…and your tenacity…and your brave heart. I have never met anyone like you."

"I love you too," she cried, a flood of tears pouring down her cheeks.

Gerald took out a handkerchief and gently dried them.

"I've gotten to know you with no memory to guide me…only my heart," she whispered, laying her hand against his cheek. "You are the kindest, most generous man I have ever known. How could I not fall in love with you?"

Selena realized they had veered down a path that had taken them to a small pond. A charming stone bench sat facing the pond, and beyond that stood a stand of leafless trees. In the time she'd been at Bellwood, she had never been to such a charming spot. "What kind of trees are those?" she asked.

"Apple trees," Gerald answered. "I discovered them the first year I was here. The horses enjoy lots of apples in the fall. But Mrs. McDonald gets the rest."

Despite the rollicking emotions she'd just felt and was still feeling, Selena laughed. "I can just see dear Mrs. McDonald wrestling those apples off the ground before the horses can take them."

"That's pretty much what happens," he said, chuckling. "Of course, I can't complain, given how much I love her apple tarts! Connery loves them too. Mrs. McDonald can't understand why her freshly baked batches of tarts constantly go missing."

Selena laughed again at the thought of the two grown men sneaking into the kitchen to steal apple tarts.

"Selena," Gerald said softly, tugging her down on the bench. "Would you sit with me?"

"I would love nothing better," she said, snuggling against his chest.

After sitting for a while surrounded by the peaceful scenery around them, Gerald leaned back and tipped her chin up.

"I love you, Selena Bowles," he said. "And I am looking forward to making you my wife one day soon. You are strong, resourceful, beautiful, and kind. And exactly who I need in my life."

"And you don't think I'm wanton?" She held her breath. How could she possibly have been so fortunate as to have found a man like this?

"No, I don't." He waggled his brows. "However, if you want to be wanton with me after we are married… You'll not receive any objection."

Selena giggled, feeling the anxiety, the pain, and the humiliation of her memory of the villainous imposter fade.

The teasing glint in Gerald's eyes changed to something warm and wonderful and romantic as he lowered his lips to hers, at first teasing her lips with feathered kisses, before covering her lips with his.

He smelled divine. His lips were soft and warm. And his touch sent flutters down her spine and across her shoulders. The warmth of his body lured her closer.

Pulling him nearer to her, she twined her hands through his brown, wavy hair and impulsively molded her body to his. This was what she wanted. This was what she needed. Gerald holding her, making her laugh, and kissing her… She closed her eyes, intent on capturing this memory in her heart forever.

CHAPTER SIXTEEN

THE SOUND OF horses and the realization they were no longer alone jolted Gerald and forced him to break the kiss. He immediately felt the loss.

"Stand behind me, Selena."

"I don't understand. Why, Gerald? Who could it be?"

He shook his head and gave her a pained expression. "Selena, I'm sorry. I'm being overly protective, and I apologize." He squeezed her hand. Hearing what happened to her had gutted him—not because he blamed her. But because he had not been there to shield her from that horrible imposter, and there was no way he would...

Before he finished his thought, a large brown gelding with a rider rode through the maze of bare apple trees, followed by several others. Gerald recognized Wright, Banbury, and his father, followed by several of the hired guards. He heaved a sigh of relief. "You gave me a start," he said, trying to relax.

"We didn't mean to startle you," Banbury said.

"But I have a lot to tell you, and none of it is good," Wright continued. "Perhaps we should head back to the house to discuss."

"We can meet in my study," Gerald offered.

A short while later, they were all comfortably ensconced in the leather seats of Gerald's study. Mrs. McDonald had already delivered sandwiches and fruit and made sure everyone had what they wanted to drink.

"I'm anxious to hear what you've heard, Wright," Gerald said to his friend.

Wright sipped his brandy and set the glass down. "Two men arrived from London within the last hour. One was with the other runners who have been watching our homes in London; the other is with the regent's men. They've spotted a man that is consistently seen with a larger man in London—specifically in Mayfair—claiming to be Lord Bowles's heir and asking questions about Miss Bowles. They appear to be trying to find your fiancée."

"The footmen turned them away," Gerald's father said. "All he would have needed was the paperwork he was given from Selena's father's solicitors to prove he was Lord Bowles, but apparently, he said he'd misplaced it."

"How convenient," Gerald growled. "The solicitors gave the official paperwork to the real Percival Bowles, so Vern would have had to steal it from him. Therefore, if he didn't have it in London, he would have to decide whether to return to Rose Point to find it. The solicitor's paperwork had to have been with him when he arrived at Rose Point." He turned to his father. "Is my assumption correct?"

His father nodded. "And I'd imagine the London solicitors that Selena's father employed would know what the real Percival looked like, so bringing one of Bowles's solicitors to confirm his identity with him also wasn't a viable option, thank goodness."

"Interestingly, they also tried to get into Lady Bowles's townhouse and were met with a similar reaction," Wright continued. "Vern claimed to be Lord Percival Bowles—but without any proper identification and a soul to vouch for him, the staff forbade him entry to the house. The footmen we hired kept him at bay, despite his threatening to bring the law in and have them all thrown out. And I'm certain they remembered how Lady Bowles arrived and realized something went very wrong in Nottingham.

They tried to apprehend him, but he must have suspected it might happen and escaped."

"One of my footmen recalled hearing Vern swearing and complaining they needed to go back to the estate, pack, and leave," Gerald's father said.

"So, if they weren't focused on finding Selena, why would they risk going to London, then?" Gerald asked—although he was already mentally going through reasons.

"He wanted whatever would have been easy pickings," Lord Bellecote replied. "He would have attempted to remove whatever of value he could from the Bowles's townhouse."

"They might be headed to Rose Point. It would take them days on horseback to reach it. Vern may have thought himself safe there. Selena told me they treated her home like a gaming hell and bordello combined," Gerald said through his teeth. "How many days ago were they in London?"

"Maybe a week…which means they may no longer be there," Wright said.

"According to Selena, he spent days drinking and carousing with the women…barmaids they hired as lady's maids and general staff from the bars," Gerald said.

"I think he's gone from London. He wasn't getting what he wanted," Gerald said.

"According to a missive I received from my butler, Forrester, the two blackguards had no idea where Bellwood was," Banbury said. "They were there for a couple of days, combing London for information."

"And the prince regent evidently dispatched a security detail to Rose Point," Lord Bellecote added.

Gerald hoped the prince regent's men were successful in apprehending the criminals at Rose Point. They would send word if they were. He thought about Selena, the woman he loved. All he wanted to do was be with her, keep her safe, hold her close, and make all her worries disappear. But he couldn't do that with her life still in danger.

"If a security detail was dispatched to Nottingham—to Rose Point—Prinny will most likely have them report back to London with details," his brother-in-law said, mirroring Gerald's thoughts.

"Wasn't a detail supposed to come here?" Gerald's father asked. "You mentioned Prinny had assigned one to protect this property."

"Yes. There are two details. However, the two security details the regent summoned were returning from different parts of England. Even so, they should be here soon," Banbury said.

"Any other news to report?" Gerald asked.

"Yes. Although I could not be completely sure based on Lady and Miss Bowles's descriptions of the criminal duo," Wright said, "my suspicions were confirmed by the descriptions from Lord Bellecote's staff and the staff at Lady Bowles's townhouse. The imposter is Vern Stiles and his enforcer is Grom Dugan. Vern is dangerous…a blighter that is always stirring up trouble from port to port. The man has been tossed off more ships than I can count. Stiles has black hair and black eyes, and Grom has shaggy blond hair and blue eyes. Grom has been known for getting into brawls at every public house and tavern in every port there is. An odd duo, to be sure. Vern would be the one pretending to be the heir of Rose Point. Grom is an extremely tall, burly individual, who towers over his co-conspirator by at least eight inches, while Vern is about the same height as we are, around six feet.

"The two of them were seen together by several eyewitnesses when their ship, the *Merry Maid*, docked in Portugal before the real Percival Bowles went missing. There have been a few allegations of petty thievery, that sort of thing—but nothing substantial. Until now. Prinny has also sent men to Portugal to investigate the disappearance of the real Percival Bowles. Unfortunately, it doesn't look good. We must assume they killed him."

"That's an interesting description of them, Wright. How do you know them?" Banbury asked.

"I don't know them, but I've seen them about on my travels,"

Wright replied. "Many times, our ships docked in the same port at the same time. I do know Percival—not well, but well enough to have believed him to be a good man."

Gerald emptied his glass of brandy and set it on his desk. "It's clear that we need to go to Rose Point as soon as possible. Hopefully, we'll get there and find Prinny's men have them wrapped up in a neat package, ready to transport to the Tower. And there may be clues as to their activities. I doubt Prinny's men were focused on much more than finding the men and will not be checking for anything else."

"If we hope to catch Prinny's men, we should leave immediately. Let's get packed and meet in the stables in an hour," Wright said.

"I'll go with you," Banbury replied.

"We can't all go," Gerald said. "I'm worried about leaving the women here, even with the additional footmen. What if something should happen?"

"I'll stay," Connery suggested, nonchalantly leaning against the door.

"As will I," Gerald's father offered. "My hair might be gray, but I can still fire a gun and throw a punch."

The men chuckled.

"Thank you both," Gerald said, feeling relieved. His father was an excellent shot, and Connery could probably wrestle a wild boar with his bare hands. If Gerald wanted to be with Selena, he had to track down those bastards and make sure they never hurt her or Lady Bowles ever again. Even if the duo had managed to avoid Prinny's men, there might be some clues at Rose Point as to their whereabouts—or what they were planning next.

CHAPTER SEVENTEEN

An hour later
Bellwood stables

"GERALD, ARE YOU sure you have to leave?" Selena asked. She had a bad feeling and couldn't shake it. The back of her neck prickled—something that always seemed to foretell bad luck.

The two of them were standing in front of Hermes's stall. The horse was already saddled and waiting.

"Aphrodite might be upset that you aren't taking her," she said, hoping to lighten the conversation.

"It was a hard decision, but Hermes needs to stretch his legs, and I won't be here for several days." He leaned down and kissed her lightly. "Selena, you have to promise me something."

"Anything… What do you want me to promise you?" She tried to be positive but couldn't shake the feeling something would go wrong. Selena had the urge to pull him close, but her mother and Connery were standing behind her, talking. She didn't want to embarrass Gerald.

"I want you to promise me you won't ride Azure without two footmen with you. I'd rather you let Joshua exercise Azure while I'm gone. It will just be for a few days. And please don't go anywhere on the estate grounds without an escort."

She was very familiar with how long it took to get here from Rose Point. She had ridden for almost two days…freezing and in the rain. She opened her mouth to say something, but closed it, not wanting to sound like a shrew.

"You will be all right, love. We won't be gone too long," he said, pulling her close. "My father will be here, as will Connery. We are taking two of the security details that Wright and Banbury hired, but that will still leave you with plenty—men we've hired and those that Wright brought. Plus, from my understanding, the prince regent has another security detail on its way from London. They should be checking in here soon."

"I'll be here, too, Lord Lawrence," Ben said, coming out of a nearby stall with Dutch right behind him. "I'll protect your home and the people here."

The dog barked, and Gerald laughed.

"Dutch! You rascal. I know you will be here, too!" Selena said, laughing. "He's been very protective of me."

"Take care of Selena for me, Dutch. I'll be back soon, boy," Gerald said, reaching down and petting the large white dog.

Dutch gave his hand a lick.

"Aye. Dutch is a warrior through and through." Connery chuckled.

"Mrs. McDonald and my wife packed some food for your journey," Ben said. "I secured it in the small satchels next to your canteens."

"That was very thoughtful of them. Thank you," Gerald said.

"I think we're ready to go," Wright said.

The men trotted out of the stables and headed for the main road. Gerald lagged behind and turned on his mount.

His eyes met hers, and Selena's breath hitched as she worried about his safety and that of the others. And she couldn't help the growing feeling that something might go wrong.

She stood with Dutch, Connery, her mother, and Ben, and watched the five men ride off. It took everything inside her not to run after Gerald and beg him not to leave, to stay with her. She knew that wasn't the kind of man Gerald was. He was honor bound to find Vern and Grom and bring them to justice.

A small tug on her dress caught her attention. Dutch looked up at her, smiling and giving her a gentle reminder of his presence.

"I know you are here, sweet boy. It'll be all right." *I'm just a little sad and scared.*

The hair on the back of her neck prickled again. Each time she felt it, she glanced behind her...but there was nothing there. Was it her instinct or was she overreacting? It wasn't surprising that she couldn't trust her own instincts, given all that had happened of late.

She recalled that Diana and Lady Bellecote were eager to decorate the manor before Christmas. That would certainly keep her mind occupied while the men were gone. She would be able to count on her mother and Maggie—and Gabby as well.

As she watched her mother drift off toward the gazebo with Connery, Selena's mind turned back to the picnic she and Gerald had shared there only days ago. It was the most special day she could remember having. So romantic. And Gerald had made it special for her. She had thought to go there herself, but not after realizing that it was her mother and Connery's destination.

Selena loved both of her parents, but her father had been much older than her mother and had been ill most of the time toward the end of his life. Even so, she had never thought about her mother finding someone else. Connery made her mother smile. She deserved to be happy.

Focused on keeping herself busy, Selena thought about what she had been working on with Diana. They were almost finished with the Christmas baskets for the tenant farmers, but surely Diana and Lady Bellecote would have other ideas about decorating for the holidays. Selena had a few ideas as well, but she didn't want to overstep. She was Gerald's betrothed, but she was not the lady of the manor yet. She would defer to Gerald's mother and Diana and offer up a suggestion here or there. The point was to keep her mind occupied. Anything to keep her busy and prevent her from dwelling on her worries and her fears. If she allowed that, she would not be able to function.

Walking into the house, she decided to seek out Diana. It was late morning, and she thought Diana might be with the babies. She did not know the woman very well, but had liked her immediately. And those babies were adorable. Selena liked everyone in Gerald's family. Gabby especially, who reminded her of herself at that age.

Lost in thought, she almost bumped into her maid. "Anna, have you seen Diana? I thought I'd see if she's up for company."

"Aye, miss. The marchioness is in the nursery with her sister and the wee ones. She mentioned it was feeding time. I just brought her a tray, so she doesn't get too hungry herself."

Selena made her way to the nursery and tapped on the door. One of the babies was already asleep in Gabby's lap, while Diana fed the other.

"Hello, Selena. Join us." Diana gave her a welcoming smile as she shifted the baby to her shoulder to burp him. "He's got a healthy appetite, just like his daddy."

"You mean he burps like his daddy," Gabby said mischievously.

Selena laughed, although she hadn't thought Lord Banbury ate any more than the other men.

"You seem preoccupied," Diana said as if reading Selena's thoughts. She reached out and gave her hand a gentle squeeze. "Don't worry about Gerald. My brother is not only brave and strong, he's clever and very resourceful—and he always keeps his promises."

"That's true," chimed in Gabby. "Gerald's been in tough spots before. But he also has Christopher and Wright by his side too."

"Perhaps I am worrying needlessly. I've spent so much time with him lately that it's hard to think of him away from Bellwood and possibly in danger." Selena fought back tears. "It's just that…that I know how cruel and evil Vern is, and he won't hesitate to kill. He was so arrogant when he thought he'd killed my mother. If not for Maggie and Ben, she probably would have died. It's just that after all these years, Gerald and I are finally getting to know each other, and I fear that something will happen to change that…"

"Come sit beside me," Diana said in a gentle voice. "I want to tell you something about Gerald. You already know him as a very caring person, but perhaps this story might help you know his character even more." She shifted and settled down with the baby once again comfortable at her breast. "I don't know if you know this, but when Christopher and I met, I had been left blind from a terrible carriage accident."

Selena gasped. "No, I had no idea, my lady."

"Please, call me Diana—we are going to be family."

Selena gave her a tremulous smile.

"It was at the end of my first London Season, and I felt so isolated after the accident. I didn't want to participate in the following Season but did it to make my mother happy." Diana smiled. "I'm afraid I kept company with the wallflowers. Yet it was when I met Christopher—but I've digressed somewhat."

"But your sight returned," Selena said.

"Yes, it did. That is rather a long story. I'll share it with you another time. But what I wanted to tell you about is Gerald and how dedicated he was to me during the most traumatic time of my life. I have a horse—Bandit—that I adore, just as you adore Azure. And when I became blind, I could no longer ride my horse. Bandit was my very best friend and I missed him terribly.

"Unbeknownst to me, Gerald had taken it upon himself to see that Bandit was exercised regularly—and Gerald rode him. He didn't relegate it to a footman or ostler. Not only did he ride Bandit, but when I came to London the following Season, he brought Bandit here to Bellwood to care for him. You see, Bandit was the first birth that I witnessed, and I raised him. Not being able to see him—or be part of his everyday existence—was horrible for the two of us. Gerald sent me updates on Bandit, telling me everything about his daily life here while I was recovering. He described everything in such detail that I felt as though I had been there to witness everything. And that is the kind of man Gerald is. I don't think I could have gotten through that very dark period if it hadn't been for him."

"Oh, Diana, I don't know what to say." Selena blinked back her tears. "Thank you for sharing your story with me. And I am so glad you are recovered and happy with Lord Banbury and your two lovely babies. Gerald and Connery took good care of Azure when I was ill after my accident. Gerald took good care of me as well. I don't know what I would have done without his strength."

"And I can tell Gerald's got his head in a spin over you, Selena," Gabby teased. "Whenever you walk into a room, he forgets we're all there."

Selena felt her cheeks suffuse with heat.

"Gabby!" Diana gently scolded her younger sister. "You're making Selena blush."

"But it's true!" Gabby said.

"Although I heartily agree with my sister," Diana said, rolling her eyes at Gabby, "I also know that Gerald will do everything in his power to catch those horrible men and make sure you are safe and protected."

Selena watched as Diana rocked the baby and wondered how many children she and Gerald might have one day.

As if reading her thoughts, Diana piped up. "Gerald has always been the best brother, and he is a wonderful uncle. He will make a very loving father, Selena. Oh, of course, he sowed his wild oats and strayed at times from what Father wanted him to do, but he's always been the caring and protective sort. When we were young, he knew how much I wanted to learn to ride. And having a brother like Gerald, who rode all the time, I wanted to be like him—and ride like him, which to me seemed effortless and carefree. It's so much less restrained than the way women must ride. I hated the way my riding instructors insisted I ride. It was my brother who taught me to ride Bandit astride."

"Really? Gerald taught you?" Selena asked, smiling now. "I love to ride astride as well. That's why Gerald thought I was a young boy when I first arrived here. I borrowed clothing so I could ride astride and left my dresses at Rose Point."

"Yes, exactly! And he found the clothes for me to wear—and made me swear I'd keep them hidden when I wasn't using them," Diana said. "He never told anyone of our lessons. My horse and I are very close, and I've always believed it was Gerald who helped me achieve that relationship. When he decides to do something, he doesn't do it halfway and he protects those he loves. It's a full commitment to do it right. Take this place." Diana waved at the room. "This estate was in a state of total ruination. He and Connery did much of the work—at least in the beginning. He appears very Corinthian, with those broad shoulders and the muscles." She gave a mischievous laugh. "Christopher must have seen my shock when I noticed my brother's new appearance, because he told me he planned to buy an ax and chop all the firewood for the country estate."

Selena snorted, and laughter filled the air.

"Seriously, I know you are worried, but they will be back. Christopher said they thought Prinny's men would be ahead of them and may have the situation well in hand by the time they arrive. Gerald's been in difficult situations. He can take care of himself. As can Christopher and Wright."

Believing Diana might think her strange, Selena decided not to share the weird, prickly feeling she had, even though it usually served as a warning for her. Instead, she forced a smile.

They spent the next hour talking about the babies and the outfits that Diana and her mother were making for Christmas. Selena found herself fantasizing about the children she might have one day with Gerald. The time with Diana and Gabby was proving to be the diversion she needed, and she found herself laughing and enjoying the funny antics Gabby shared about herself and Gerald.

She silently prayed that Gerald and the other men returned safely…with Vern and Grom in shackles.

CHAPTER EIGHTEEN

Rose Point Chateau
Nottingham, England
Two days later

"THE PLACE APPEARS to be eerily deserted," Gerald said, running his hand through his hair. "Which means what?" The other four men pulled up alongside him, and the small party continued to move slowly as they progressed onto Rose Point's grounds. They'd thought there was the possibility they'd face some sort of fight. Instead, they faced destruction…chaos.

"Good God!" Wright said as they took in the smoldering piles scattered across the grounds in front of the manor house. "They've burned furniture, clothing, linens. It's almost like the man is set on punishing the Bowles family. What kind of person impersonates a man to steal everything of value, yet leaves a trail of destruction behind?"

"A narcissistic, crazed person," Banbury said in a grim tone. It's conceivable he may not have found what he was looking for and decided to burn things in a fit of pique. As you know, we've seen worse."

Gerald knew his brother-in-law and his friend had seen depravity and destruction in their work. The marquess had worked for the Crown. And Wright occasionally worked alongside friends who still worked for the government—in one branch or another—doing reconnaissance. The Napoleonic Wars had ended, giving rise to riots and fears of conspiracy.

Banbury had been an indispensable agent, having saved the prince regent's life on more than one occasion, earning Prinny's undying friendship. Gerald was thankful his brother-in-law had given up that dangerous line of work and was now happily settled with Diana, raising a family, and managing his estates and investments. It was what he wanted most as well. Spending time with Selena had only solidified that for him. He wanted to spend the rest of his life caring for her, giving her babies, and expanding his stable of racehorses.

"I wonder if Prinny's detail caught them and are on their way back to London or if they ended up giving chase," Gerald said.

"Possibly," Banbury replied. "Although Vern and his minions certainly took the time to destroy as much as they could."

"Then again, this could also be the work of vandals who might still be inside. Let's proceed with caution, gentlemen," Wright said.

"It hasn't rained in the last two days, so it's easy to see tracks in the driveway." Gerald pointed to the tracks of horses. "Perhaps Prinny's security detail was here. That's a lot of horse tracks. It's impossible to say how many men, but it's too many for just two."

Once they caught the bastards, they would have to look to restore all the damage done to the estate. He would do everything in his power to assist Lady Bowles. He was positive Connery would be leading the way. Gerald couldn't help but notice the burgeoning friendship between the two. Under better circumstances, he would be teasing Connery about it. Gerald had seen the way the Scot looked at Lady Bowles when he thought no one was paying attention. He was happy for his friend. Connery deserved to be happy—God knew the man had suffered enough in his life, losing both his wife and child.

"Well, gentlemen, I think it's time we ventured inside," Banbury said.

"No matter what we find," Gerald said in a steely voice, "leave Vern to me." Everything Selena had told him was burned in his brain. He would not rest until Vern was captured.

"Let's start with the bedchambers and work our way down," Banbury suggested. "It's conceivable we might find something of importance there as to their whereabouts."

The men quietly made their way upstairs. They fanned out, each taking a bedchamber to search. Gerald instinctively knew when he entered Selena's room. The evidence of the vile invasion was everywhere. The armoire was empty of gowns, no doubt stolen by the crude women Vern had given free rein to. The window curtains had been yanked down, the delicate wallpaper had been shredded, and bed linens had been ripped and strewn about. The vanity had been toppled over, and drawers from the dresser had been taken off their tracks and tossed to the floor. Despite the destruction, Selena's lovely floral scent still lingered. He breathed it in and took strength from it.

Selena had told him about the secret passage, and he wondered if he could find it. Crouching down, he ran his fingers along the bottom of the bookshelf and felt a catch where the shelf met the wall. He pressed it and watched as the passage sprang open. It appeared Vern had never determined there was a secret passage. The man probably assumed she had jumped from the window to the sturdy branch of the tree that stood outside. Gerald shuddered as he imagined the terror Selena must have felt to leave in the middle of the night, alone, with only her horse. Leaving her mother's supposed grave unseen. She was the bravest woman he had ever known.

Having found the passage and seeing little use now for it, he closed the door and continued to poke around the room. He spotted an empty brandy decanter on the fireplace mantel, and an empty bottle of gin under the bed. He felt another wave of anger knowing that Vern and his friends had been in Selena's room and defiled it. Thank God she was safe at Bellwood.

As he made his way into the hall, he saw Banbury emerge

from the master bedroom. "Anything?" he asked.

"Nothing but lots of empty liquor bottles and decanters. The man had an unquenchable thirst, it seems," Banbury said in a disdainful tone. "From all the bottles we've seen up here alone, it appeared he and his friends must have guzzled everything in the house and probably whatever might have been in the cellar."

The other men emerged from the rooms, all shaking their heads.

Despite the destruction and disarray, they'd found nothing to indicate where Vern or Grom might be.

"I've seen no evidence anyone is still here...so far," Wright said as they made their way back down to the main floor.

"I'm surprised there are still so many paintings still hanging," Gerald observed. "Although it looks like some didn't make it through the last party." He pointed to a pile at the end of the hall. "Let's start with the study."

The study, like the rest of the house, was a shambles. Drawers were pulled out, books were thrown and scattered all over the floor, and bottles were smashed.

"It appears he was looking for something," Banbury said. He pointed to the open safe—the door was still hanging open. "Lady Bowles said he made her give him the combination."

Gerald felt an almost menacing presence in the room. He silently fumed as he recalled Selena's story. Vern had terrorized her and her mother. No woman should have to endure such treatment. He silently swore he would make Vern pay.

They continued to sift through papers and books, searching for something that could tell them what Vern was planning.

"He might be insane, but he's a clever bastard," Gerald said. "He knew his impersonation of Percival Bowles could not last more than a few months at best."

"True, and he couldn't just go to London to meet with the solicitors to get his greedy hands on Bowles's money. Such actions would be questioned by the solicitors, and he couldn't risk that," Banbury added.

"Nor could he sell any paintings or furnishings," Wright said. "There wouldn't be time for that. Not to mention he would be drawing attention to himself."

"Eventually word would get out," Gerald said.

"There are enough people out there who know what Percival looks like, including myself," Wright added.

"But as we've seen, he stole all the jewelry they had in the house—he could make his escape with that," Banbury suggested.

"True, but it would still take time for him to sell it on the black market," Wright said. "Yes, there are pirates who will take jewelry as payment, but they would most likely slit his throat while he's sleeping."

"And there weren't enough funds in the house for him to be able to plan his escape to God knows where," Banbury said. "So, what is there left for him to do?"

Gerald saw the corner of a document that had slid to the floor peeking out from under the desk. He picked it up and skimmed it, shouting a curse as everything crystalized in his mind. "It's our betrothal contract. Mine and Selena's." He held it up for his friends to read. "He knows!" he shouted. "Damn it to hell. He knows. Selena is to inherit her grandmother's estates and money on her twenty-first birthday. It's right here plain as day in the betrothal contract." He raked his hands through his hair. "Her birthday is in two weeks! He's planning to kidnap her. We've got to get the hell out of here and back to Bellwood."

As they made their way out of the study, they heard a vase topple over and footsteps running down the hall. Alarmed, Gerald and his friends took off after the intruders.

They followed the thieves to the kitchen. Signaling to Wright and Banbury, Gerald entered the kitchen on stealthy feet. He could hear crying and whispering that sounded like it was coming from the larder—a room with the door standing propped against the wall. It must've gotten in someone's way and they saw fit to rip it off—like so many other doors and drawers Gerald's group had seen since their arrival. He stepped inside, scanning the almost empty larder, and in the far corner huddled behind a pile of empty baskets, he saw them—a little boy and a little girl. Their tear-stained faces were stark with fear as they clung tightly to each other.

"Well, who do we have here?" Gerald asked, a little more abruptly than he intended as Banbury and Wright entered right behind him. The little girl began to shake even more. "What are your names?" he asked in a gentle voice as he crouched down.

The little boy pushed the little girl behind him as though protecting her, then stood with his shoulders straight, as though willing to take any punishment on her behalf. "M'name's Paul and this be m'lil sister, Kat," he said in an accent that sounded slightly Cockney.

"Where are your parents, Paul? More to the point, why are you here?" Wright asked.

"Our mum brung us here when she got off work at The Pig and the Poke. She said there would be nice things for us and plenty of good food to eat. When we got here, there weren't much in the way of food. I managed to find us some apples. Mum told us to stay put and went off with some bloke. She were laughing with him, and he passed her a bottle of whisky as they left. Kat and I waited and waited until we fell asleep, and when we woke, everyone was gone."

"Where do you live?" Wright asked.

"Makes no difference now. We never had one place to live. Mum was always moving from village to village. I guess she got tired of bringing us along with her." The boy's lower lip trembled as he spoke. "I'm taking care of my baby sister. Our mum don't want us."

"How long have you been here, Paul?" Banbury asked, softly crouching next to Gerald.

"Maybe four days," the little boy said. "Like I said, we ate what we found on the tables, but t'weren't much."

Gerald looked at the children. They were severely malnourished and clearly in need of a bath and care. Anger roiled in his belly. What kind of mother would treat her children like that and then abandon them? "We don't mean you any harm. Would you allow us to help you?" he asked. "We have food with us, and warm blankets. We can take you to my home, where we can help you."

Paul turned to his little sister and whispered in her ear. She whispered back.

"All right, we'll go with you, milord," the boy said. "But please feed Kat first—she hasn't been feeling too good."

"I promise you that we have more than enough food for both of you," Gerald said gently.

They helped the children out of the hiding place. Gerald picked up Kat and carried her in his arms, and Banbury held Paul's hand as they walked back out to their horses, where their footmen were waiting.

Wrapping the children in blankets, they fed them from their supplies and gave them water.

"Don't feed them too quickly or give them too much water at once—these children are starving, and it could make them ill," Banbury said quietly to Gerald.

"Paul, could you answer a few questions for us?" Wright asked as the children ate.

"Aye, milord, I will if I know the answer."

Wright's lips twitched. "Have you seen a man with long black hair and coal-black eyes? He's fairly tall like us, but he is with a man who is much taller and has long, blond, shaggy hair."

"Yes, guv'na. I saw them. They left just before the soldiers came."

"He must mean the security force," Banbury said in measured tones. "When did the…soldiers get here, son?"

"Three days ago. They looked everywhere for the man with the bigger man, but Kat and me stayed hid from the soldiers. Mama always said never to get caught by soldiers or they'd take us to Newgate."

"Where did you end up hiding, in the larder?"

"No, milord, 'twere in the stable… We burrowed under the straw in a corner."

"The two men, the bad men. Did you happen to overhear them talking before they left?" Gerald asked, not expecting an answer.

"Yes, he was angry," Paul said, tugging his sister closer. "He said the chit was as good as his."

A cold dread shot through Gerald. This confirmed his suspicions. They had to get back as soon as possible. "Thank you, Paul—you and Kat have been very helpful." They bundled the children up and took them with them on their journey back to Bellwood.

The bastard was most likely hiding in the woods beyond Bellwood, waiting for his chance to strike. Gerald prayed they could get to Selena before Vern did. Judging from what was done here, everyone was in danger.

Bellwood Plantation
The next day

SELENA KICKED HER covers off. She felt restless and nothing seemed right. Gerald had been gone for days, and she worried that they had encountered Vern and Grom and God knew who else at Rose Point. What if there had been a confrontation? What if Gerald had been wounded or worse? And the prince regent's men hadn't arrived to assist them, as Banbury had said they would. Had something happened to the soldiers? Had Vern managed to kill them?

Logically, she knew she was overreacting. After all, Connery was here, and Lord Bellecote, along with the additional footmen who were spread out guarding the estate. But try as she did to dismiss her imaginings, she couldn't leave them be. Her mother had always told her to trust her instincts. She'd wanted to speak to her mother about her fears, but she did not want to intrude on her newfound friendship with Connery. Her mother had been through so much that Selena wanted her to be happy and enjoy her time with the tall, rugged Scot.

The only thing that helped to calm her fears was Azure. His presence always soothed her.

"Anna, I'm going to the stable to visit Azure," she said as she finished dressing. "He's probably ready for more treats."

"Yes, miss. I saw a stack of apples Mrs. McDonald brought up from the larder. Perhaps she'll part with some of those for your handsome horse," Anna replied, chuckling as she tucked the clean sheet onto the mattress. "I'd be happy to ask one of the footmen to go with you. Lord Lawrence said not to go out without an escort."

"I'm sure Connery and Ben are in the stable. I should be fine."

Anna gave her a look. "Miss Bowles, I know you've been feeling prickly since Lord Lawrence left. I'd be happy to fetch a footman to go with you."

"I'll take Dutch with me." The dog had taken to sleeping next to Selena's bed at night. "Surely he'll be a good escort to the stable."

Anna shook her head. "I think you should do as Lord Lawrence asked," she said. Dutch's ears perked up, and he angled his head as he regarded both women. "But it seems your mind is made up, and I can see that your escort is ready and willing to assist you, milady," she said, laughing again.

Selena left the house with several apples tucked in her pocket and Dutch at her side. "Azure will be thrilled to have the apples, Dutch. And I am thrilled to have you by my side. I know you take your job as my protector very seriously."

"Rrrrrruff!" the dog barked, in obvious agreement.

Selena felt that odd prickly feeling again and looked around her. There was a slight rustling of some shrubs across the field. It was probably a rabbit or a fox, she reasoned. "I swear, I think I see Vern Stiles everywhere. How ridiculous is that, Dutch?"

"Rrrrruff!" the dog barked, and smiled at her.

As they entered the stable, she saw Ben feeding the horses and felt a sense of relief. "You're getting an early start," she said, smiling.

"Miss Selena, you are here bright and early to see your horse. I just fed him, but if you've got an apple in that pocket of yours, I know Azure will jump right on it."

"You know me. I can't resist giving him a treat."

"Well, he adores you for it!" Ben chuckled. "If ye need anything, Miss Selena, I'll be over there doing some repairs."

"Thank you, Ben." She smiled as he hefted a toolbox and began to make his way to the other end of the large stable.

Selena touched the apples in her pocket. When she got to Azure's stall, she climbed up on the gate and leaned over. "Hello, handsome!" she cooed.

The horse whinnied.

"I brought something for you," she said.

"And I've brought something for you," a familiar voice said from behind her.

Dread assailed her as she slowly turned. "Vern!" she gasped. "He...mumph..." Selena opened her mouth to scream, but he clamped a hand over her and stuffed a foul-tasting rag in her mouth. He tied another rag around her head, making it impossible for her to speak.

Dutch, who had been visiting Aphrodite, ran to Selena and began to growl at the stranger.

"I see the secret is out," Vern huffed, pulling her in front of him as a shield to keep the dog at bay. "Even if I'm not going to be Lord Percival anymore, I've got everything I need to secure my future...you!" he whispered in her ear.

Selena mumbled through the gag. Her worst fear had been realized. *Please, someone help! Gerald. Gerald, I wish you were here...*

"And you thought you were smarter than old Vern." He pulled a rope from his pocket and wound it around her arms and torso, immobilizing her, then pushed her to the ground. She could do nothing but watch helplessly.

Dutch flew into action, sinking his jaws into the murderer's leg and shaking it. Blood oozed from the wound. Dutch refused to let go. Vern kicked out and then hit Dutch with an iron rod. Selena screamed through her rag as she watched the loyal dog fall.

She tried to roll into Azure's stall but couldn't move. Surely Ben would hear the commotion and come to her aid.

She could smell smoke in the barn and began to panic, kicking and trying to get up.

"Yes, that's smoke you're smelling. This whole place will soon go up in flames. But don't worry," Vern said with a sneer. "I'm going to take you and your fine horse with us. He'll bring a pretty penny." He tried to grab Azure's reins. But the horse reared up, crashing against the stall. He kicked again and broke the latch, opening the stall's door.

"Fine! No matter. You're what I wanted. I came for you, sweet Selena." Turning her over to face him, Vern withdrew a bottle from his pocket and poured it onto the rag over her face. "This will calm you down. And keep you from fighting me. The horse would have made a nice profit, though," he said, hoisting a weakened Selena over his shoulder. Seemingly unfazed by his bloodied leg, Vern carried her to a horse that he had hidden behind a stand of shrubs—the same shrubs she had seen move earlier.

She thought she recognized the horse as one of Gerald's but could no longer be sure, as the sickly smell of laudanum invaded her senses. She felt nauseated and lightheaded. In what seemed like seconds, everything started to turn dark. Selena thought she heard Azure's furious cries in the distance as the smell of smoke began to grow stronger. She tried to stay awake, but it was impossible as everything faded to black.

CHAPTER NINETEEN

GERALD RODE INTO Bellwood and noticed the smoke coming from the direction of the stable. "Dear God! We're too late... He already got to her, and the stables are on fire!" Squeezing his legs, he spurred Hermes to pick up the pace as they rode. As he approached the manor house, he saw his staff had already formed a human chain from the well to the stables and were dousing the flames. He spotted more people running out of the house to help but didn't see the person his heart needed to see.

"Selena!" he yelled. "Selena...where are you?" Even as he shouted her name, he knew she wasn't there. He felt the agony of loss from the depths of his soul.

"We have to help put this out first," he said, "Selena could be inside." Gerald slid from his horse and helped Paul down. Banbury climbed down with Kat, who was asleep in his arms. Wright had already run ahead to help.

"You have to stay here with your sister—out of harm's way," Gerald told Paul. Then he spotted Connery emerging from the burning building carrying a bloodied animal. "Dutch!" The dog's eyes were closed. Gerald tried to form coherent words. Except for his horses, he had never had a pet before Dutch. "My God! Is he..."

"He's alive. I've sent for Dr. Baker," Connery said. "I suspect the pain knocked him out."

Banbury and Wright ran toward the line of people putting out the fire as Gerald and Banbury spoke with Connery.

"What happened?"

"I heard screaming…" Connery began. Before he could finish his sentence, Lady Bowles ran up to them.

"I heard the alarm and came running to help. Please let me help," Selena's mother cried out.

"Where is Selena?" Gerald demanded. A stark fear coursed through his body and his heart threatened to burst in his chest.

"She's been visiting Diana and the babies in the mornings," Lady Bowles said, her eyes wide and filled with fear.

"Is my wife inside with the children?" Banbury asked.

"Yes, I just came from there; they are safe with Lady Bellecote, but I came out to see if I could help."

"My lord, my lord," Anna called out, running up to them. "Selena came out early this morning to feed Azure. She had Dutch with her… Dutch has been sleeping by her bed every night since you left, milord. He followed her everywhere."

"She went out with Dutch, and no one saw her?" he questioned. "No one was with her?"

"No, milord. I suggested she take a footman with her…" Anna began, and stopped. Squaring her shoulders, the petite woman said stoically, "No, milord. I let her go without an escort. I am so sorry. I failed Miss Selena."

"It's all right, Anna. It's not your fault. She had Dutch with her and thought she would be fine, and he valiantly tried to save her."

The young maid nodded, wiping tears from her cheeks.

A sob escaped Lady Bowles, and she turned to Connery. "Oh, Angus, my daughter is missing. What can we do?"

"Gerald will find her and bring her home," he said. "Everything will be fine, I promise."

Paul ran up behind Gerald and tugged on his shirt. "Mr. Gerald? Can we help? I've toted water before," he said. "Kat and me…we want to help."

"Who is this?" Connery asked, nodding at the children.

"We found them at Rose Point, hiding. Their mother left them… It's a long story. We can sort it out later."

"I'll take Dutch inside and tend to his wounds as best I can before Baker arrives," Connery said. "Fleur, come with me, and we can help these children get out of harm's way. I'll be back as soon as I get the children settled. Anna, you can help us."

Anna nodded and rushed forward. Banbury handed Kat to Anna as Fleur took Paul's hand. Connery, Lady Bowles, and Anna rushed toward the house with Dutch and the children.

Gerald took a steadying breath as he realized Selena was truly missing. There was no longer any question. Vern and Grom had her, and there was no telling what was happening to her at this very minute. Several days ago, when he'd turned around to wave goodbye, he knew from her expression that she was begging him to stay. At this minute, he wished he had. *I'm so sorry, Selena. I'm going to find you, no matter where you are. I promise with all my heart. I'm not going to lose you.*

His father and Ben rushed out just as he and Banbury were nearing the stables. Wright had already run inside.

"Ben was there when it happened," Gerald's father said, panting from the exertion. "Ben, tell my son what you know."

"You were in the stables when this happened? What did you see?" Gerald asked.

"I saw Miss Selena—she was with Dutch, visiting with Azure. I had some work to do at the other end of the stables. But as I was working, someone came up behind me and hit me, milord. When I came to, I saw that Selena and Azure were gone and Dutch was lying in a pool of blood. I found Azure running around outside the stable in a frenzy. When I was able to secure Azure, this was what I found on the ground next to him." The older man withdrew a delicate white shawl from his coat pocket and handed it to Gerald. "I think he took your new mare. It's the only horse that's missing."

Taking the shawl, Gerald swallowed past the large lump in his throat. All he could think about was that his dear, beautiful Selena was in that vile man's hands, fighting off God knew what. "Thank you for the information."

"Son, do you know where he might have taken her?" his father asked.

"I have a theory—"

Sudden shouts came from the barn. Wright and Banbury were dragging someone out. The man appeared to be unconscious. Gerald ran up to the men, followed by his father and Ben. The unconscious man was a giant. "Who is he?" Gerald rasped, trying to slow down his racing heart.

"It's Grom," a stranger's voice said from behind them.

Gerald spun around to behold a tall, dark-haired man striding toward them, flanked by two men on each side.

"Who the hell are you?" he demanded.

"I'm Percival Bowles."

There was a moment of stunned silence before Wright said, "I'm glad you're not dead, my friend."

"So am I, believe me," Percival replied in a grim voice. He ordered his men to help with the fire. Ben went with them.

Gerald immediately noticed the stitches on the side of Percival's head. "Did they do that to you?"

"Yes. I had just been having dinner at the tavern with Captain Davies and First Mate Winters in Lisbon, near the port. Our ship had just docked. A fight broke out at the bar. It started with two men but escalated quickly into a melee. And when there's a brawl in a port town, you can't just leave. We ventured in to try to stop it, and before I knew it, someone had hit me from behind. I woke up with my hands and feet tied, under the docks. It was still low tide, but I knew I didn't have much time before it started to rise. I managed to remove the bindings on my hands and feet and then pulled myself up to the docks just as the tide was rushing in."

"My God, man, you are one lucky son of a gun," Wright said, slapping Bowles on the back.

"Aye, I certainly am."

"What happened next?" Gerald asked. "Did you notify the authorities?"

"I did, and they said it would be next to impossible to find out who was responsible. I was incapacitated for nearly a week with this gash on my head while the authorities, along with my captain and first mate, investigated and spoke to the owners of the tavern and various other possible witnesses. Unfortunately, port cities are what they are—people either lie or don't speak up when they witness a crime."

"The prince regent sent a contingent of men to Portugal—did they make contact with you or your captain?" Gerald asked.

"Yes, when they arrived, they informed us about a man who'd taken my identity to lay claim to my inheritance. They described the man and his cohort, and we knew immediately who they were. I came here as soon as I could, as you see, with men from my ship."

"Well then, you can help us get the truth out of this bastard," Gerald said, kicking the sole of Grom's boots. "I need to know where Selena is. Throw some water on him and wake him up!"

Wright retrieved a bucket of water and tossed it over Grom, causing the giant to sputter and groan.

Gerald grabbed him up by his shirt. "Where is she? Where is Selena?"

"He took her," Grom rasped.

"Did he take her to Gretna Green?"

Grom groaned as he nodded. "He's going to marry her to steal her inheritance."

Gerald's fists clenched as he let out a low growl of fury. He was itching to give Grom a thrashing, because he couldn't hit Vern. Because he hadn't stayed here instead of taking off on a wild goose chase to Rose Point. And because his heart ached to see Selena's beautiful smile and hear her beautiful voice. He missed her more than he thought he could ever miss anyone.

But he balled his fists up and shoved them in his pockets. The man would swing soon enough. And Gerald wanted every bit of information he could find out about Selena and that filthy imposter, Vern.

Blood streamed from various wounds on the giant's arms and shoulders. He appeared to have been stabbed several times.

"I didn't want him to hurt her and tried to stop him," Grom said with a groan.

"Last I heard, you were part of his evil plans. Where did this sudden attack of decency come from?" Wright asked.

"I never wanted to hurt anyone, but I didn't stop him either. I couldn't. He kidnapped my thirteen-year-old sister and said he would sell her as a slave if I didn't do what he said. Once I got here, the foul little toad stabbed me. When I get my hands on him…" The man's words died on his lips in the face of Gerald's anger.

"You won't have to." Gerald felt a steely calm invade every fiber of his being as he stood up. He knew what he needed to do. There would be nowhere the bastard could hide. "I'm going to kill him," he said.

"Oh, no you don't," Percival said. "You can't divorce yourself so easily from his acts of betrayal. You're telling me he kidnapped your sister? When did he do this, and how do we know you're telling the truth?" he asked Grom.

"All of it was Vern. The man's the devil incarnate. He threatened to sell her if I didn't help him with this. And he said he'd make sure she got broken in by the ship's crew first. My God! You know what they do to women on slave trader boats. She's only thirteen! I've been trying to find her—hoping he will get drunk enough to tell me or find something that will lead me to her. Angela's never done anything to hurt a soul." Grom looked up at Percival. "I'm sorry for what I've done, Lord Bowles," he croaked. "He told me to drown you, but I couldn't, so I left you under the docks. I thought you would be able to free yourself before high tide."

"I'm having a hard time believing you to be a saint in this.

What else can you tell us?" demanded Wright.

"He has a carriage," replied Grom. "It was hidden in an abandoned barn about a half-mile up the road from the estate. We watched the guards and snuck onto the estate when they didn't see us."

"Describe it…describe the carriage," Gerald said, grabbing him by the collar.

"Black…shiny. The inside is red. Vern stole it from an inn on our way. It has four brown horses," groaned Grom. "All I've told you…'tis the truth."

The sounds of horses' hooves sounded from behind them, and they all spun around to see almost a dozen men, all dressed in royal uniform, riding onto the estate.

"Finally! The regent's guards," Gerald murmured. "Too late to help Selena."

"Keep your temper, son," his father said. "They can be of help, here and with you. The horses have all been saved, and the damage to the barn was contained to the back." He nodded toward the house. "Your mother and Lady Bowles have the children and women in hand. Hear what the guards have to say. Maybe they have more information."

"Doubtful, Father. I'm not sure how Vern and Grom slipped away from them to begin with. Make sure the guards hold on to this one," Gerald spat. He inclined his head toward Grom before walking toward Hermes.

"We're coming with you," Wright said.

"Take as many men as you need," Gerald said, climbing onto Hermes. "You'll have to catch up to me."

Selena, I'm on my way, love. Don't lose faith.

CHAPTER TWENTY

Somewhere on the road to Gretna Green
Just before dawn

THE DAY HAD turned cold and brutal with rain and wind, and Gerald was reminded of what Selena must have gone through when she fled Vern. He, Percival, Wright, and three of Wright's men were on Vern's trail. Banbury had stayed behind to assist with the cleanup of the stables and make sure the women and children were all right. Gerald had not worried about leaving Banbury, along with his father and Connery, to oversee every-thing. He knew they, as well as the regent's men, would continue to question Grom. Dr. Baker had arrived just as they were leaving. The good doctor would tend to Grom's wounds, but the giant would be kept in the cellar until they returned.

After riding for the rest of the day and most of the night, they weren't any closer to finding Selena. Gerald was beyond frustrated. They had stopped at every inn along the way and questioned the innkeepers and their wives, and any servants in case they might recognize the description of Vern and Selena.

Gerald was determined to find her. But how could Vern be that much farther ahead of them? The barn hadn't been on fire that long, so he couldn't have had that much of a head start. "We've not missed a single inn on this road. So far, we've turned up nothing. There are absolutely no signs of the bastard," he said to Wright.

"There is one more inn on this stretch of road, and then a mile-long stretch with no other establishments. It's a pity we don't have a better description of his carriage. I'm sure Vern didn't dispose of the horse he stole. So that may be tied behind it."

"Sounds like you've traveled this road a bit," Gerald said.

"I've traveled it a time or two, but not for the reasons you think," Wright replied. "Usually looking for someone else's sister or loved one."

"Ah, Wright, you'll forever be the last bachelor standing, eh," Percival teased.

"Why should I limit my charms to just one lovely lady when there are so many who yearn for my attentions?" Wright replied. "Poor Percival—now that you're a newly minted viscount, you'll no longer be able to travel from port to port wooing those luscious senoritas. You'll have to take your rightful place among the *ton*, manage your estate, marry a dewy-eyed debutante, and spend the rest of your life landlocked."

"I only just got here. I haven't even been to Rose Point," Percival said. "Besides, there will be a lot to sift through after all this is over. Finding a dewy-eyed debutante is not exactly first on my list."

"All right, you two, before you launch into tales of your romantic exploits, shall we get back to our search?" Gerald said dryly.

"I believe there is one more inn in this area before a stretch of highway and the next batch of inns," Wright said. "If I recall, it's just around the bend. I won't pretend to know the name of it."

"Either Vern greased their palms or threatened the innkeepers. There's no way he could be traveling in a carriage with Miss Bowles and not have stopped," Percival said. "Unless these innkeepers are the same as the ones I'm used to dealing with in port towns."

"People elope to Gretna Green, so innkeepers and tavern owners are used to keeping silent about the couples who stop for the night. I suppose it's part of the culture here," Wright added.

"That must be the inn up ahead," Gerald said, pointing to a white building with heavy smoke coming from its chimney, just as they rounded the curve in the road. "Let's spread out," he said in a low voice. "We'll cover the front door and the back so the bastard can't escape. Look for the carriage."

Gerald and Percival went in, while Wright and one of his men watched the front, and Wright's two other men went to the back. It was the same routine they'd followed at every stop.

Gerald strode up to the innkeeper and began to ask if the man had seen Vern and Selena. He went on to describe Selena and what he knew of Vern.

"No, milord. We've not seen anyone that matches that description," the innkeeper, a man named Lampshire, said, shaking his head.

"Have you seen a black carriage with a red interior come through this day?" Gerald persisted. Looking around, he saw several black carriages, although he'd have to get closer to see if their interiors were red.

Still, the man shook his head.

Gerald's gut told him that the innkeeper was lying. "Mr. Lampshire," he said, "are you married? Do you have children? A daughter, perhaps?"

The balding, stout man nodded. "Aye, my wife Margie and my daughter Helen."

"Then you understand how important it is to protect the women we love from evil predators and criminals."

The innkeeper heaved a deep sigh.

"This brute kidnapped my fiancée. He's wanted by the authorities in Portugal and England for both murder and attempted murder. He won't hesitate to do it again. She is in grave danger. Surely you, as a husband and father, understand how devastating it would be to lose either your wife or daughter to such a vile man as this."

Still, the man shook his head.

"Aye. We saw them." An older woman stepped out from the kitchen. "I'm Mrs. Lampshire. Please don't be angry with my husband. He was threatened by that devil. But seeing you gentlemen here, I believe in doing the right thing."

"What can you tell us?" Gerald asked.

"The man said it was their honeymoon and 'e didn't want to be disturbed. He was coarse and ugly. I would never have put a lovely lass with such an ugly old toad as that one. He handed my husband a few gold coins and then turned around and threatened us."

"Margie, hush," the innkeeper said.

"Giles, we have to help that lovely girl."

"All right," Lampshire said. "My wife is right. He threatened us. He's a mean son of a bitch. He said if we told, he'd burn down our inn."

"But if he tries, I'll have my blunderbuss Bess waiting for him," Margie said.

"What room are they in?" Gerald asked. When a second ticked by with no answer, he repeated the question, this time in a thunderous voice. "*Room?*"

"Oh, for God's sake, Giles." The man's wife flipped open the registry and read through the names on the list. "M-milord, it's the honeymoon suite, room 201 at the end of the hall," she said.

Gerald took the stairs two at a time with murder on his mind.

"I SHOULD HAVE taken you when I had the chance," Vern said, stalking her to the other side of the large room.

Selena was standing in the corner gripping a chair in front of her as a barrier. *My God! How could this have happened?* Her life had become a living nightmare once more. She whipped her head around the room. What could she use as a weapon? But she could see nothing. Perhaps she could lift the chair. But it was too heavy to wield.

She'd been so happy in the days she'd spent at Bellwood. Despite her worry about Vern being out there, somewhere, she'd felt loved and cared for. Gerald had lived up to every girlhood dream she'd had about a knight in shining armor. He was kind and loving and made her laugh and was so handsome she could swoon. His family had welcomed her with open arms. She felt that she truly belonged, that her future with Gerald was something bright and full of light and love. But Vern had found her. Somehow he'd slipped past the footmen and kidnapped her. And now she was once again alone, facing her worst nightmare. She wished she could close her eyes and wish herself back to Bellwood. But she couldn't afford to close her eyes, not even for a second.

She trembled as she pressed against the wall. Vern cackled like a demon as he reached out and flung the chair away. He pressed himself against her and grabbed her by the throat. "I can't wait to make you mine, my beauty." He bit her shoulder, making her scream as he dragged her to the bed. She tried to push him off, but he held her arms over her head in an iron grip as he yanked up the hem of her dress.

"No, leave me alone!" she screamed. Thrashing back and forth, she managed to free her leg and knee him in the groin.

He howled in pain as he rolled off her.

Selena scrambled off the bed and frantically searched for something she could throw at him.

"Oh, I see you like it rough," he rasped. "We'll be married soon enough, and it won't matter if I take what should have been mine weeks ago…so let's make it now. After all, this is the honeymoon suite."

He grabbed her once again. Foul whisky breath washed over her, and she gagged at the stench. She had to fight. She could not allow him to assault her. To steal the precious gift reserved for

Gerald. Tears came to her eyes as she remembered his kisses, the touch of his hands, his smiles, his tender words…

Vern caught her by the hair and dragged her back to the bed. Throwing her onto the mattress, he tore at her dress, exposing her legs and thighs. "That's better," he muttered. "Happy honeymoon, my dear little wife. After we marry and I get my hands on your inheritance, you'll die in an unfortunate accident, and I'll be so grieved I'll have to leave the country."

"You vile beast," she shouted, spitting in his face.

"Bitch!" He backhanded her, and Selena fell onto the bed, dazed.

Suddenly the door to the room was smashed open and the heavy weight of Vern disappeared. Trembling, she sat up and saw Gerald appear as if from a dream, slamming a bloodied Vern against the wall.

⟶⟩⟩⟩⟨⟨⟨⟵

"SAY YOUR PRAYERS, you bastard," Gerald growled, wrapping his hands around Vern's throat.

Heavy footsteps sounded from the hall and Wright ran in. "Stop, Gerald. You can't kill him."

Percival followed Wright into the room. "My lord, you must let justice see him hang."

Both men tried to pull him away, but Gerald tightened his hands around Vern's neck.

"Gerald, my love, please stop…" Selena's faint voice reached his ears. Slowly reason returned and he slammed Vern against the wall.

He turned and rushed to Selena, who was sobbing on the bed. Gathering her into his arms, he hugged her fiercely. He pulled away and regarded her face. "My God, what did that bastard do to you?" he rasped. Her face and throat were black and blue, and blood was pouring down. He pulled a handkerchief from his pocket and gently cleaned away the blood, looking for the source of the wound.

"I think it's from a cut above my eye," she whispered.

Gerald carefully dabbed at the cut, trying to stop the flow of blood. He knew from experience that cuts above the eye bled profusely.

"You make a habit of coming to my rescue," she murmured.

Gerald chuckled softly as he continued to tend her wounds. "My love, I will gladly spend the rest of my life coming to your rescue," he said tenderly.

"I hope you won't have to. I hope this is finally over," she said, her eyes filling with tears again.

"It's finally over, my love, I promise. I promise. I promise," Gerald said, his voice catching as he pulled Selena into a tight embrace and rocked her while she wept into his shoulder.

CHAPTER TWENTY-ONE

Bellwood Estate
Derbyshire, England

AFTER WHAT HAD occurred two days earlier, Gerald was unwilling to leave Selena's side. By the grace of God, they had found her, and he wanted nothing more than to spend every minute with her. If they had arrived any later, Vern would have…

A tremor shook him. He couldn't even finish the thought. It had all been too close.

But with both his parents and Selena's mother in residence, Gerald reasoned he would have to be content with checking on her. When he stopped by her room on his way to breakfast, he was told by Anna, whom he passed in the hallway, that she was still sleeping, exhausted from the horrible ordeal. He nodded and waited until the maid had left, then he opened the door to Selena's room and walked in.

Spying his dog at the foot of her bed, he couldn't help but envy Dutch, who lifted his head and regarded him silently. The dog's eyes showed an almost human-like ability to convey a promise that he would guard Selena with his life.

Gerald patted the dog's head and sat in the chair next to the bed. Leaning over, he smoothed his hand over Selena's soft, silky hair.

When did you become so important to me? When did my life become so inextricably linked to yours?

From the moment he picked her up after she tumbled off Azure's back the night she arrived in that rainstorm, and those incredible blue eyes of hers gazed at him before she fell unconscious, he'd known that his life would never be the same again. As each day passed, he'd found himself bemused, enchanted, and charmed by the essence of Selena Bowles.

But, he could admit to himself, his connection to Selena had begun long before that night. It had begun at the Adamsons' ball five years past, when he met Selena for the first time. She was barely sixteen years old, and he was a very foolish, headstrong twenty-two-year-old. He remembered how slender and frail she seemed, how innocent, how delicate. At the time he thought she resembled a lost little bird. Fool that he was, he'd failed to see the beauty she would become. But even back then, her remarkable eyes had held him captive.

He wondered if the past five years of rebuilding Bellwood and launching his racehorse enterprise had only been about proving himself to his father—or was it also about Selena? Maybe, deep down, he'd known that his connection to Selena went beyond a betrothal document. Maybe he'd been driven by the beauty and the whisper of who she would become—the courage and strength that had always been inside her.

And maybe he'd had to prove it to himself. That he was a worthy man.

Selena stirred and breathed a deep sigh in her sleep.

"Sleep, my love. We'll talk later," he whispered as he stood and placed a soft kiss on her brow. After lifting the covers up over her shoulders, he turned and made his way downstairs to the breakfast room.

"How is Selena, darling?" Lady Bellecote said, setting down her cup of tea.

"She's still asleep," he said. "It could be the combination of fear at having to fight for her life and the laudanum that was so liberally administered by that demon. Honestly, I can only be thankful she was still able to fight him. Mayhap she experienced some sort of rush of blood or heightened sense of energy in the moment she needed to fight him. I'm no man of science, but I'm happy for whatever it was that sustained her. Once she realized I had her and she was safe, she could barely keep her eyes open." If Wright hadn't stopped him, Gerald might have killed Vern Stiles. But his friends were right—he needed to let justice take its course. Killing the scoundrel would have furthered that demon's control over their lives.

"And you—how do you fare this morning, son?" his mother asked. "We've all been concerned about Selena, but we are worried about you as well."

"In this moment, just knowing she is safe and back home is enough for me, Mother. I appreciate everyone's concern, though." He nodded for the footman to fill his cup with coffee.

"Son, no one would have anticipated Stiles coming here and kidnapping Selena. Do not blame yourself," Lord Bellecote said.

"I know, Father, but it was my duty to keep her safe, and I didn't." Gerald clenched his jaw, and his fury flared anew as he remembered breaking into the room and witnessing Selena at the mercy of that bastard. "I'm just relieved it's over and she's back home."

But now he had other worries. What if Selena was emotionally scarred by the kidnapping and being attacked by Stiles yet again? What if she never forgave Gerald for not being able to protect her? He prayed that she would. And he would do everything in his power to help her heal.

Following a brief knock, Wells stepped into the room. "My lords and ladies, Lord Wright has returned with Lord Percival Bowles and Baron Alfred Jones, our local magistrate."

"I'll meet with them in my study," Gerald said. "I've been anticipating their return." He turned to his father and Banbury. "Will you join me as well?"

The two men nodded and followed Gerald to his study.

"What's the word on Grom?" Gerald asked after Wright, Percival, and Jones had joined them.

"According to Captain Livingston of the regent's security contingent, Grom confessed to quite a bit; however, the man still insisted that he was forced to participate because Stiles had abducted his thirteen-year-old sister, threatening to sell her into slavery," Wright said.

"Indeed. But Stiles inadvertently substantiated Grom's story when baited, so that was added to his growing list of evil deeds, and there is a sense of urgency where the girl is concerned," Baron Jones began. "The prince regent's men are working with the authorities in Lisbon. Reportedly, she is outside the town, perhaps in a nearby village, hidden in a house or a barn some-where. The reason we know this is that the local authorities believe there is a connection between the abduction of Grom's sister with the abduction of several other girls in the area. Evidently, at least ten girls have gone missing in recent months, one of whom is the granddaughter of a powerful nobleman in Portugal. The authorities in Lisbon have already been searching, and we have every reason to believe that they will recover the girls soon."

"He is working with a pirate by the name of Blackjack Ow-ens," Percival added. "They've worked together before. Stiles, as you know, was working on board my ship. He kidnaps girls from towns and villages nearby whatever ports our ship docks in, and then keeps them prisoner, in a remote location. Once he captures enough girls, usually ten or twelve, he transports them to Blackjack Owens, and they sell the girls on the black market. It's heinous. And we've been trying to stop this for some time. Stiles has always been one step ahead of us. But now, we've got him."

"Are you saying that that was the reason why Stiles had Grom try to kill you in Portugal?" Gerald asked.

"He knew we were onto him," Percival said. "We were fol-lowing him to see if he could lead us to where he was keeping the girls. When Stiles found out about my inheritance, he thought he could kill two birds with one stone, so to speak. His intention was never to actually become the new viscount, but to try to steal as much as he could from the coffers and then join up with Blackjack again."

"And was Grom involved in all these despicable crimes? Banbury asked.

"No," Percival replied. "We found no evidence of this. Stiles was working on his own with Blackjack for many years. Grom had been his own man, working on board various ships for several years. Because of his size and strength, he was always in demand."

"Grom had a good reputation up until he met Stiles," Wright added. "He was always known as a gentle giant."

"Until Stiles joined the crew of my ship, the *Merry Maid*," Percival said. "Likely, he found out about Grom's sister and kidnapped her to force Grom to do his bidding."

"And while Grom denied trying to kill Selena, or physically harming her in any way, he acknowledged that he was forced to be a party to what happened to Lady Bowles—as he was the one who obtained the poison," Wright said.

"That, alone, could get him the noose, although he risked his life to stop Stiles's attempt to kidnap Selena and burn the barn," Percival said.

"We all know Vern Stiles is capable of anything," Gerald replied. "When he came across the betrothal agreement and realized that Selena was an heiress in her own right, he clearly thought he could get his hands on a treasure by forcing her to marry him. He knew that he couldn't keep up the charade forever. There were bound to be people who knew what the real Bowles looked like, but by kidnapping Selena and making for Gretna Green, he thought he'd landed his golden goose."

"Thank God you got to her in time, son," his father said.

Gerald nodded. They were lucky indeed, but he would never allow himself to fall into that kind of trap ever again. Selena and his family were the most important people in his life. He would always do everything in his power to protect them.

"What will happen to Grom?" Banbury asked.

Jones cleared his throat. "Apparently the regent may consider his attempt to stop Stiles. They will also take into consideration his previous upstanding reputation and the fact that Stiles kidnapped his sister and coerced him."

Wright turned to Gerald. "Would you object to Bowles and I speaking on behalf of Grom to the regent?" he asked.

Gerald paused and took a deep breath. "I believe both of you and trust your judgment. I think the true evil force at work is Stiles."

Percival nodded. "I agree. I thank you for your support in this matter."

"Where are Stiles and Grom being held?" Gerald asked.

"The prince regent's men are transporting Grom to the Tower today, along with Stiles," Jones replied. "Both men are heavily chained to avoid any chance of escape. There was another witness to Stiles's treachery—one who is willing to testify. During their initial search for Lord Bowles, the prince regent's men questioned some of the workers at a nearby bar, and a barmaid spoke up. It seems she knew the two of them well. According to her testimony, she was tired of Stiles's threats, and whenever he was in port, he made lives, including hers, miserable with his treachery. And while I find her willingness to testify against such a vile man unusual, considering the tendency toward vengeance the man exhibits to those who cross him, her testimony may be the final nail in his coffin. Stiles will be in solitary confinement until his trial. He will soon see his last. His fate is sealed at the end of a noose. His list of crimes is a mile long."

"I absolutely agree," Banbury said. "He is too dangerous to be considered even for transport to Australia."

"I think we owe ourselves a brandy after all of this," Gerald's father said, pouring them each a glass.

A thoughtful hush fell over the room as everyone took a quiet sip.

"That is all I have to report for now," Jones said, breaking the silence. "Thank you for the brandy. I shall keep you all posted on any developments. Now, I must take my leave, gentlemen." He inclined his head and left.

"Damn," Gerald said, blowing out a breath. "What a twisted web." He wanted to share everything he'd found out with Selena. He'd promised to always tell her the truth. But given what she'd been through, he would have to tread carefully. The last thing he wanted was to add to her pain.

CHAPTER TWENTY-TWO

FLEUR SIGHED AS she watched her daughter sleep. Selena had been napping on and off since Gerald rescued her. It would take a few days for her to regain her strength, and until then, Fleur would be by her side.

"I should have taken better care of you," she whispered, smoothing back Selena's hair. "I should have known that he was an imposter from the beginning and had Ben go for help."

"Maman?" Selena's eyelids fluttered open.

"My darling girl. How are you feeling?"

"Better. It's good to be home."

"It's good to have you home."

"Maman, please don't blame yourself."

"You heard what I said? I thought you were still asleep."

"Yes, I was just waking up and heard you. None of this was your fault. How were you to know? How were any of us to know that Vern was an imposter? But it's over now, and we can get on with our lives."

"You are such a brave young woman," Fleur said, blinking back tears. "I'm so proud of you. So very proud."

"Oh, Maman, I'm proud of you too. He tried to poison you and you survived. If it wasn't for your insisting that I escape, I still might have stayed there. I guess we proved to ourselves how strong we truly are."

"Now we're both crying, *ma chérie*," Fleur said, reaching for a handkerchief and gently wiping her daughter's tears.

Selena shared with her everything that had happened from the moment she was in the stables to when Gerald and the others rescued her.

"I don't remember much after that. I think I slept the entire way home."

"Are you happy here, my darling? Are you happy to be with Gerald?"

"Oh, Maman, I love him so much. I can't wait to marry him."

"Good. That fills my heart with joy. I can see how much Gerald adores you too."

Selena blushed as she beamed at her mother. "He's everything that I hoped he'd be and more."

"I'm so happy for you."

"Thank you, Maman. Thank you for being such a wonderful mother to me."

"It has been the greatest joy and privilege of my life, my dear daughter."

They reminisced for a while, sharing happy memories from Selena's childhood when Phillip was still a strong and vibrant man.

"Your papa loved you so much," Fleur said, caressing her daughter's cheek.

"I know, Maman. I loved him too."

"I remember when you were a little girl, you used to look at him like he'd hung the moon and stars."

"He did," Selena whispered. "For me, he did. He always will."

"My darling, there is something I wanted to talk to you about."

"Yes, of course."

"Once you are feeling stronger, and once we have settled Paul and Kat into their new routine here, I'd like to go back to Rose Point to help Percival put the estate back in order," Fleur said. "He invited me to help. He said he doesn't know the first thing about managing an estate and asked for my assistance." She had felt pulled in several directions—should she live here, or in London, or move back to Rose Point? But Rose Point was her home, and with Selena now safe and in the care of her fiancé, she felt compelled to see to her own circumstances. Of all their properties, Rose Point had always been the one nearest and dearest to her heart. It was the place she and Phillip had called home. And it was where Selena had been born and raised. "How do you feel about that?"

"I want you to live with us, of course, but I know you will be able to help Cousin Percival—although from what I know of him thus far, I'm certain it would not take long for him to learn all that he needs to know. Then you can come back here and live with us."

"Well, Percival also has plans to expand the dowager house on the estate to make it more comfortable. I would live at the manor house and help guide him, and then, when the dowager house is renovated, I would move in there."

"But Maman, what about when I become *enceinte*?"

"Darling, nothing could keep me from your side with each child you bring into this world. I will come here and stay with you as long as you like." Fleur leaned over and kissed her daughter's forehead. "I promise you, my darling, I will always be there for you when you need me. But I know how important it is to have privacy when you are a young married couple. And you will have a ready-made family. Paul and Kat need you and Gerald. And trust me, you will cherish those first years of your marriage—more so without relatives around every day." She chuckled.

"I have only just met the children, but I am already in love with them," Selena said. "When Gerald told me about them, I wanted to meet them immediately. I cannot believe their mother abandoned them. It is beyond cruel."

"Darling, not every woman has the love and ability to be a mother. Giving birth to a child does not make you a mother.

Raising a child does."

"But I will always need your guidance."

"And you will always have it. But I have seen you with those children, so patient and kind. You have that gift, my darling." Fleur and Anna had brought the children to visit with Selena as she recuperated. Selena had read to them and taught them songs from her childhood. The children had been instantly drawn to her. Kat had laid her little hand on Selena's cheek and asked her if she was a fairy princess. And Paul, who had been so stalwart and stoic when they first arrived, gazed at her with such adoration, it had warmed Fleur's heart.

Selena sighed. "But what about Connery? I thought that you were becoming close friends…"

Fleur felt the heat of a blush stain her cheeks. "Indeed, we have become close. Connery has spoken to Gerald about going to Rose Point as well. He has offered to help guide Percival in estate management. Gerald readily agreed."

From the start, Fleur had been drawn to Angus—to his strength and sense of honor. Every time she looked at the tall, ruggedly handsome Scotsman, she felt like a young woman in the first throes of love.

At first, she'd felt a wave of guilt at her growing attachment to him. But then she remembered how her late husband had encouraged her to embrace life after he was gone. They'd had many conversations in those final days after he'd had his heart attack. She had been so lucky to have been able to say goodbye to her beloved husband. And she had been moved by his wish that she find love again.

"We have had a good life, and I have loved you with my heart and soul for all the years we've been married," Phillip had told her, *"but after I'm gone, I want you to keep living…"* Fleur had tried to stop him from saying what she knew he was going to say, but Phillip had placed a finger on her lips. *"Hush, my darling, and listen to me. You are a vibrant woman with so much to give. Please do not waste the life God has given you grieving me for the rest of your days. I want you*

to find a man who will give you the happiness you deserve."

Fleur had sobbed as she'd lain next to Phillip in those last days. At the time, she could not see a future without him, so embedded was she in her grief, but after his passing, as time marched on, she felt the warmth of his blessing and wisdom urging her to live and be happy.

"Maman, I know how much you loved Papa," Selena said, bringing Fleur back from her memories, "but I want you to know that I am so happy for you. Connery is a fine man, and I know he makes you happy."

"Thank you, my darling girl. My heart feels a little lighter at hearing you say those words." Fleur hugged her daughter and told her she would be back later. Connery had asked her to go for a walk, and her heart was aflutter at the thought of spending private time with him.

ANGUS STEPPED OUT of the stables and saw her standing a few feet away. Fleur was kneeling as she warmly greeted Dutch. The dog wagged his tail in excitement. "I know just how you feel, Dutch," he murmured. Fleur looked as pretty as a spring morning. She was wearing a blue gown that made her beautiful eyes sparkle like sapphires. She fairly took his breath away. Now that the worst was behind them, her smiles came more easily, and whenever he heard her tinkling laughter, he was drawn to her like a moth to a flame. Hell, he'd been attracted to her from the start. The fact that she seemed to enjoy his company left him a little in awe.

"Good afternoon, Fleur," he said as he approached her.

"Angus," she breathed.

Ach, but she is a beauty. "You look lovely this afternoon."

"Thank you."

"Shall we go for our walk?" He offered her his arm and they began their stroll, Dutch trotting behind them. Angus wanted to take her to the winter garden that Gerald had planted. Located behind the manor, the garden was visible from Gerald's study. He'd claimed he wanted something peaceful to look at when he needed a break from tending to his estate ledgers, but Angus knew he now wanted to be able to gaze at Selena as she enjoyed the garden. Gerald had begun work on the garden well before Selena arrived, yet his attention had meandered in no real direction—but after that fateful night when Selena arrived, he had thrown himself into finishing the garden. Angus had offered to help the young man, sensing Gerald's determination to finish it for Selena, and marveled that they'd completed it in record time. Then again, a man could move a mountain if he had to for the woman he loved. Angus felt the same way as he led Fleur to the white bench beneath a jasmine-covered pergola facing the garden.

"How beautiful! I didn't realize you had a gardener," Fleur said, leaning down and smelling the bounty of white, rose-like flowers. "Camellias are one of my favorites."

Angus grinned. "We do have one, thanks to one of the tenants. But the gardener didn't do this. Your soon-to-be son-in-law did. He painstakingly searched for flowers that would thrive in winter, including those snowdrops you see over there, but it may be a few more weeks before they make their presence known. He had planned to put in pansies before Selena went missing. According to Gerald, he's re-created a design that his grandfather created for his grandmother. He told me he spent many days as a young boy learning how to garden from his grandfather."

"I can see how much love he put into it. The garden is beautiful."

"I see it as a sign of hope," he said in a gruff voice. "Winter brings harsh weather and cold days, but knowing this garden is here makes you realize that life goes on, that no matter how dark and dreary it is, there is still beauty in the world."

"What a beautiful sentiment," she whispered. "You are a man of poetry, Angus Connery."

He chuckled. "Well, I'm not sure about that, but I thank ye for the compliment."

"I am in awe of this garden," she said. "It seems my son-in-law has an abundance of talents. Is that winter jasmine covering the stone border? We have it growing at Rose Point." She took a deep breath, inhaling slowly. "This garden is a breathtaking sight, with the most glorious scent. And with vibrant pansies and delicate snowdrops, I can only imagine the beauty when it's all in bloom."

"Yes, it is jasmine. Except for the pansies, the rest are perennials and will return year after year. I'll only have the pansies to find," he said. "I helped a wee bit, but I do enjoy coming here and wanted you to see it."

"Thank you for bringing me," she said softly. "Angus, I just want you to know that I am so happy you're going to be at Rose Point to help guide Percival."

"As am I. Not because I don't have faith that the young Bowles is incapable. I've only known him a short while, but he seems to be as capable as Gerald. And with everything he's been through, I am glad to help."

"But that's not the only reason why I'm happy you're going to Rose Point," she continued. "I'm happy because I'll get to spend more time with you."

Angus reached for her hand and brought it to his lips. He touched them to the pulse point on her wrist and felt its fast flutter, like the wings of a bird. "That is my fondest wish as well."

"I spoke with Selena about moving back. I told her you were going as well."

"And what did she say?"

"She is happy for me. I no longer have to worry about my daughter. She is stronger than I thought, and she has Gerald and now Paul and Kat. They are creating their own little family."

"Are you saddened that she no longer needs you in the way that she used to?" he asked.

A tear squeezed out of the corner of her eye, and he caught it with his thumb. "I was at first. What mother doesn't grieve when her child grows up and leaves the nest, so to speak? But these are tears of joy as well. I know my daughter is happy and in love. And I know that Gerald returns that love. He will make a fine husband."

"I agree, they are an exceptional couple."

"I also spoke with Selena about you."

"Oh...?" he asked, trying to sound nonchalant, even though his heart was hammering in his chest.

"Yes. Do you want to know what we talked about?"

"Do you want to tell me?"

"Angus, you can be quite stubborn sometimes." She giggled.

"Is that what you talked about? My stubbornness?"

"No, I told Selena how happy I was that you were also going to be moving to Rose Point to help with the estate."

"Ah, I see."

"But that's not all. I also told my daughter how much I cared about you."

Angus shifted on the bench to look into her eyes. "I can't tell you how much it means to me to hear you say that. Because I care a great deal for you as well." He tipped up her chin and slowly bent down to claim her lips.

"Lady Fleur Bowles?" he said in a raspy voice after their kiss.

"Yes, Mr. Angus Connery?" she whispered.

"I think this is the beginning of a beautiful relationship." And then he bent and kissed her again.

CHAPTER TWENTY-THREE

Bellwood Estate
Two days later

GERALD KNEW SHE would be here. He knew Dutch would be by her side. Dutch had been his dog and now was devoted to Selena. He didn't mind. Not one bit.

Selena was whispering softly to Azure as she fed him a carrot. Gerald had so many things he wanted to say to her, but there was one very important thing he had to say first.

"Good morning," he said as he approached her.

"Good morning," Selena said, turning to him with a soft smile.

"How are you feeling this morning?"

"Better. So much better than I was yesterday, and much better than the day before," she replied.

Gerald took her in his arms and placed a gentle kiss on her forehead. "I have something to ask you."

"Is everything all right?" she said, eyes wide with concern.

"Yes, everything is fine. Dr. Baker stopped by to check on Paul and Kat. They are on the mend. I swear, between Mrs. McDonald and Maggie feeding them, Anna and Gabby reading to them, and our mothers and Diana sewing clothes for them, they will be right as rain in no time."

"Love and time will heal their wounds, both inside and out," Selena said softly. "They are lovely children."

"I know. You've been spending a lot of time with them as well."

"I can't help it—they are so adorable."

"Yes, I agree."

"I don't remember them as the children of any of our tenants," Selena said. "Paul told me that his mother was a barmaid at The Pig and the Poke, but that they had been traveling from town to town since Kat was born. I shudder to think what would have happened to them if you hadn't found them at Rose Point. Thank God you did. What will happen to them, Gerald?"

"As you know, Paul told us his mother abandoned him and Kat. I believe him. I have no desire to go searching for a woman who would do such a vile thing—and who might in turn try to extort money from us. When Paul is older, I will help him find his mother, should he wish to do so."

"Does that mean what I think it means?" she asked.

"What do you think it means, my darling?"

"Do you want Paul and Kat to stay with us? Because if you do, I would be so happy."

"I do," he replied. "And I'm glad you're happy. I want us to raise them as our own."

"Oh, Gerald, you are the kindest, most incredible man in the world."

"Well, if you say so. Who am I to argue?" He grinned, bending down to kiss her. "I have something else to tell you. Percival and Wright set out early this morning to assess the damages at Rose Point. It will require a lot of work—that bastard really did a lot of damage."

Selena gave a deep sigh. "Yes, Maman already spoke to me about it. She mentioned that Maggie and Ben would be going with them. They'll be of tremendous help, and I'm sure they will be able to track down many, if not all, of our former staff members. While I am deeply saddened that Rose Point was ravaged by that evil man, I have every faith that Percival will restore it to its former beauty."

"And how do you feel about your mother moving back there to help?"

"I'm happy for her. She has a renewed sense of purpose. Maman will give Percival all the benefit of her wisdom." She smiled. "And how do you feel about Connery moving there?"

"I'll miss that rough old Scotsman, but I'm of the same mind. He will be able to guide Percival in the same way he guided me."

"I'm happy for them. For Maman and Connery."

"Ah, so you've noticed as well?"

"Noticed? It's as plain as day how much they care for each other!" She giggled. "Maman smiles like a debutante with her first crush when she talks about him. She deserves to be happy. She is still young and has many years ahead. I would not want her to spend those years alone as a widow. Besides, I know she will always love Papa and keep him in her heart. She seems years younger since meeting Connery." Selena leaned in close to whisper to Gerald, "And I've noticed she's always blushing when they return from one of their afternoon walks."

"Connery is the same. I think they'll almost be as happy as we are."

"Ah, you don't say…"

"I do say." Gerald bent down and claimed Selena's lips in a passionate kiss. "Actually, I have something else I wanted to speak to you about."

"My, you have quite the list this morning," she teased.

"Yes, I do," he said, chuckling. "I've had thoughts about Azure and possibly other thoroughbreds."

"And what are those thoughts?"

"Azure is one of the finest horses I've ever beheld. For you to have ridden him here alone makes him a very special horse. And you have a special rapport with him," he said, gazing into her lovely eyes. "Connery was right—you have an uncanny ability to understand animals. I was planning to ask for your assistance in helping me expand my stable of racehorses."

"You mean help you train them?"

"Yes, that is what I mean."

"Oh, I would love to. I know I have a lot to learn—"

"My love, while there is much I can teach you about the industry of horse racing, I believe you have all the inherent talent you need when it comes to training animals. I've seen the way you communicate with Azure and the other horses and Dutch. You are extraordinary."

"Thank you," she said, a lovely blush tinting her cheeks.

"I want you by my side, helping me expand this venture and making our stable of racehorses the best in the country."

"Gerald, I am—I don't know what to say. That you would ask me to work with you… I am so touched and honored."

"Nay, it is I who is honored by having you in my life and by my side," he replied. "Diana is a very accomplished horsewoman. And I feel certain Gabby will be just like her. She's been begging me to let her ride Aphrodite."

"Oh, goodness! You don't plan to allow…" She stopped. "I sound like my mother did when my father brought me Azure."

His laughter filled the air. "No, not until Aphrodite is much calmer. You have nothing to worry about there. And I'd welcome your help with her. She's still a bit wild. The race at Newcastle will be in May. I'd like to race Hermes and Aphrodite. And possibly one more. I will be hiring jockeys to train with them shortly. But in the interim, your help would be invaluable." Selena's interests were so closely aligned with his own. *If only I'd spent time with her sooner.* Instead, he had neglected their engagement for all those years until disaster almost took her away from him.

"I've had some thoughts on things along those lines, too," she said. "I truly enjoy spending time around horses. I would love to ride with Diana, but her time has largely been taken with the children, so we aren't able to spend much time together. And—"

Gerald gently placed a finger over her lips. "My darling, you don't have to feel bad about that. With Mother and Gabby here, she's had plenty of help." He wrapped his arms around her. "I'm so glad you're safe and back here with me."

"Oh, Gerald, I'm so sorry I didn't listen to Anna and take a footman with me when I came out here the day Vern snuck into the stable." Selena nodded in the direction of Dutch, who was dozing on the soft hay about ten feet away. "I almost cost that sweet dog his life with my foolish behavior." She shivered, and Gerald held her closer. "It's really over? That evil man is out of our lives?"

"It is, my darling. You won't have to worry about Vern Stiles ever again. You have nothing to fear from that blackguard for the rest of our lives. Both my father and Banbury, along with Percival, will be speaking to the magistrates and Prinny himself to make sure they know the extent of his crimes, including the kidnapping of those poor girls. And Prinny was livid about that, not to mention the fact that Stiles tried to kill a peer of the realm. He will be tried and hanged for his crimes, you have my word."

"What a vile and evil man. What about Grom? Is he also going to hang?"

Gerald let out a deep sigh. "I don't think so. Percival and Wright have offered to speak on his behalf. Because of the extenuating circumstances with Stiles coercing him, I think they will be lenient. Percival also mentioned that he wants to take Grom under his wing, promising the magistrate that he will offer the man employment and maintain contact with the authorities on Grom's behalf."

"That is very good of him," Selena said. "I think he is a good man. My father told us he had every faith in Percival before he passed away. And that evil imposter will be punished as he should be."

Azure gave a resounding whinny as though in agreement.

"Yes, Azure, I know how you feel about that horrid man." She smiled as she petted his mane.

"Now, for the final item on my list of things to ask you,"

Gerald said.

"Oh my, is it last but not least?"

"It is definitely not least."

"Very well, I am all ears."

Gerald reached into his waistcoat pocket, withdrew a small box, and dropped to his knee in front of her.

Selena's eyes widened, but she stayed quiet.

In that tranquil moment, Gerald found the courage he needed to speak the words he had rehearsed in his head. "Selena Bowles, for years I ignored our betrothal, believing I had been wronged by my father to have been committed to a future wife at such an early age. However, little did I know back then—I was a fool, by the way—that the most incredible woman in the world that I would ever hope to meet was right there all along. I thank God for your courage and strength in riding through a rainstorm in the dead of night to reach Bellwood. And since that fateful night, I have gotten to know your heart, your bright and clever mind. I have been mesmerized by your beauty, both inside and out. And I have been captivated by those incredible blue eyes. I have come to realize the wisdom of my father, and yours, and how they wisely had our best interests at heart. And with all of this, I hope you will consent to be my wife. I love you, Selena. And I will love you forever."

As Gerald finished his heartfelt proposal, he opened the black velvet box and displayed a gold band with a large sapphire stone surrounded by small diamonds. The ring sparkled in the light, drawing a smile from her lips.

Selena's azure eyes sparkled with tears of joy as she flung her arms around him with such fervor, she nearly toppled them both to the ground.

"I think that bodes well," he said, laughing.

"Yes, it does, my love! Oh, Gerald... Yes, yes, a thousand times yes!"

As their lips met in a searing kiss, Gerald thought he was the luckiest man in the world.

EPILOGUE

Bellwood Estate
The week before Christmas
One year later

S ELENA PICKED UP two baskets she had prepared for the tenants
and moved them to the pile in the corner of the kitchen.
Looking at the one she'd just finished—full of fruit and cheese—
she gave a satisfied sigh. They had been a lot of work, but so
worth it. At almost nine months into her pregnancy, she felt like a
waddling duck. Only a month earlier, she'd started acknowledg-
ing she was in her confinement. From Selena's perspective, it
made things go more quickly.

"Darling, you may continue to work on the baskets, but I
must insist you allow me or one of the footmen to move them,"
Gerald said, entering the kitchen and kissing her on the cheek
before taking the baskets from her. He placed them on a nearby
table. "Dr. Baker relented to allow you to walk around instead of
the standard bed rest, but you need not overtax yourself."

Selena blew out a big sigh. "I'm ready to deliver this child,"
she admitted. "I walk like a duck, and I feel like a cow."

Despite being warned by both his father and brother-in-law,
Gerald laughed. Banbury had been the most recent to warn him
about the frustrating, self-deprecating comments that women

made in their final months of pregnancy, but still, Gerald took the bait. And Selena immediately turned and gave him a teary-eyed response—one Banbury had also warned him about.

"Am I fat and ugly in your eyes?" she sobbed as heavy tears crested over her lower lashes and rolled down her cheeks.

Damn! I'm going to have to dig myself out of this one with wit and charm. "No, darling. You are carrying our child and are the love of my life. And you could never be anything but beautiful," Gerald said, kissing her nose. Using his handkerchief, he wiped her tears away. "It'll soon be your birthday, darling. I want to spoil you."

Hiccupping through her tears, she said, "And you love me like this?"

"Selena, I find you to be the most beautiful woman in the world," he said before covering her mouth with his and kissing her ravenously. "I love you."

When he finally pulled away, his wife reached up, wrapped her arms around his neck, and pulled him closer. "It's just it's been uncomfortable to move and sit and sleep these past few weeks," she said. "And as much as I love carrying our child, it feels like I can't get close enough to you, Gerald. I know I'm being ridiculous, but I cannot seem to help these feelings. Diana was right. I've become a watering pot these past few days. She told me that her emotions escalated during the weeks before she gave birth and warned me that I would most likely feel the same." She rested her head against his chest and then pulled back and looked up at him.

Affectionately, he tapped her nose with his index finger. "*That* is probably why Dr. Baker wanted you to stay close to the house and recommended bed rest. You've been busy of late, but now the nursery is complete. The baby has piles of new clothes, all washed and folded. You've even hired a nanny. From a planning perspective, I think we're ready."

Her mouth formed a large O, while her eyes still brimmed with tears. Despite that, she smiled. "I will rest more. I promise. I'll just finish packing the baskets and let you and the footmen move them."

He grinned. "I can agree to that. By the way, I almost forgot the reason I came to the kitchen. My family just arrived. Mrs. Evans is helping to get them settled, and I told her I would watch you and make sure you weren't overdoing it."

"I heard from Maman earlier today, too. She said that she, along with Angus, would be here with Paul and Kat today. I'm grateful they took the children for a visit at Rose Point."

"Me too—it gave us the chance to get everything ready for Christmas."

"Maman mentioned that she and Connery had a surprise to share. I truly enjoy surprises, especially on my birthday," Selena remarked. "This year, we have much to be grateful for. Your horses have done so well." Both Selena and Gerald were thrilled when Aphrodite placed second at Newcastle and Hermes won at Epsom Downs.

"Yes! And you helped so much with the training. I'm almost certain we couldn't have done as well had you not worked your magical gift."

"It's not a magical gift," she said with a roll of her eyes. "I simply talk to them." To her, it seemed a natural skill. But Connery and Gerald touted it as something special.

"Well, you were invaluable in helping us choose that gray mare. She is the perfect mate for Azure. Their offspring will be fine thoroughbreds. Connery and I are looking forward to seeing the foal and seeing if it looks like its sire."

"I'm so proud of you, darling. Papa would be thrilled to have been involved. He loved horses," Selena said. "He gave me my first pony when I was four years old. Or maybe I was three. In any case, Paul and Kat will love the ponies you purchased as their Christmas presents."

Anna stepped into the kitchen. "My lady. Lady Bowles, Mr. Connery, and the children have arrived. I've shown them to their rooms. Since the nursery has been set up for the new baby, I've placed Paul and Kat in the room next to the nursery and moved the small twin beds into the room." Dutch trotted in behind her and curled up next to Selena.

"That's a wonderful idea, Anna. I appreciate your thoughtfulness," Selena said. "With Christmas a week away, there's so much to do."

"You may be welcoming your baby soon, my lady," the maid said, giving her a knowing grin.

Selena let out a tired chuckle, her swollen belly making any movement a struggle. "It will be both a relief and a joy. Walking is an effort. Well, if you can call this walking. It feels like waddling to me," she remarked with a weary but warm smile. "Can you let me know when Maman has settled into her rooms?"

"I will, milady," Anna said, broadening her grin.

A few minutes later, Mrs. Evans and Mrs. McDonald bustled into the kitchen and insisted that Selena take a break, something she was relieved to do. Her mother and mother-in-law had already volunteered to help deliver the baskets. Although Selena would miss traveling to the tenants this year, the jarring ride in the wagon would probably send her into labor, and she had no desire to have her child born in a wagon. Gerald had promised they could do a mid-year delivery of gifts for the tenants, and she'd been satisfied with that. It would be a nice surprise to do this again in six months.

"Mrs. Evans, do you still need help finishing decorating the Christmas tree? I'm available," Selena said.

"Oh, yes. I could use as much help as possible," Mrs. Evans replied. "I've placed the string and cranberries in the family room near the tree."

Since last night, Selena had felt more than a little bit of pressure to finish decorating the house. She had had a dream in which she delivered her baby. While she couldn't recall the sex of the child, she vividly recalled becoming a new mother.

"Happy birthday, *ma chérie*," her mother said, kissing her on the cheek.

"Maman! It's so lovely to see you," Selena said. "Thank you

for the birthday wishes."

"Did I hear you ask about decorating the tree? You know how much I love to do that."

"I did," Selena said, smoothing her hand over her stomach. "I want to make sure everything is completed before the baby is born."

Her mother's gaze moved over Selena's belly. "When did you say your baby is due? It's possible you may share a birthday."

"I suppose that's true. It's due anytime now," Selena said. "And I'm ready for him or her to arrive."

"I know exactly what you mean," her mother said, taking a seat next to Selena and picking up a string. While Selena and her mother threaded the cranberries for the tree, Selena tried to relax, but a nagging pain in her back had started. Worried, she scanned the room for Gerald and saw Dutch trot in and move next to her, behaving as though he were simply trying to find a comfortable spot to lie down, but she knew him better than that. Dutch was as sneaky as he was brave and loyal. "I know what you're doing there, Dutchy, sniffing at those bowls when you think we're not watching," Selena said. "What about all those treats Mrs. McDonald baked for you?"

Dutch tilted his head and gave her a little woof.

"Don't look all innocent with me," she said. "I'm keeping my eyes on you."

The big dog huffed out a breath and retreated a few feet to a safer location just in front of the cheery fire in the large hearth.

After an hour, she and her mother had strung several strands of garland. Selena reached into the bowl and noticed it was empty. Laughing, she realized Dutch had indeed managed to sneak into it while they were decorating the tree. But her laughter slowed as the persistent pain in her lower back became sharper.

"Maman, I think this baby might be coming," she whispered in between short breaths. Increasing pain made speaking difficult.

"Let me help you stand. I think we can make it to your room," her mother said.

"No, Maman, I'm too heavy with child. You must send for Gerald." Selena tried to get up but lost her balance and fell back into the chair.

In that instant, Gerald entered the room carrying a newly filled bowl of cranberries. "I thought you ladies might need more. It always disappears quickly, as we eat as much as we string…" His eyes fell upon Selena, who winced. "My God, Selena, what's wrong? Is it the baby?" He dropped the bowl and rushed to her side, kneeling before her.

All Selena could do was nod as another sharp pain took hold.

"Gerald, thank goodness, I was just going to find you," her mother said.

"When did the pain start?"

"Only a few minutes ago," his mother-in-law said.

He yanked the rope for a footman. "Send for Dr. Baker, and hurry," he ordered the man who walked into the room only seconds later. Gerald scooped up Selena in his arms and climbed the stairs to their bedroom.

"Please don't leave me alone," she said as he gently laid her on the bed. "They may tell you that you cannot stay, but you must. Promise me. I'm so worried something will go wrong." The only person that made her feel safe was Gerald.

"I promise, sweetheart," he said, squeezing her hand and kissing her forehead. "I will not leave your side."

According to Mrs. Babble, the midwife, who'd arrived the day before in anticipation of the birth, the husband's staying was highly irregular. But Gerald refused to leave, holding Selena's hand and whispering loving words whenever she needed comfort. The verbal tug-of-war ended with a loud "harumph" from the wiry, white-haired woman, who threw up her hands in frustration when Gerald threatened to send her packing. She chose, instead, to assist Dr. Baker—who had arrived and taken over her efforts.

SEVERAL HOURS LATER, a throaty cry sounded from Gerald and Selena's bedroom. The room was abuzz with activity, and Gerald was completely in awe. He marveled at the strength of his beautiful and delicate wife to push something the size of a pumpkin from her person. It wasn't that he hadn't witnessed births, but they had been horses or dogs. Never had he seen a woman give birth to a child—and Selena had just given birth to *his* child. His love and admiration for her soared as he beheld her strength and courage throughout the labor.

Holding his son in his arms, he had to blink back tears.

"You did it, my darling wife."

"We did it, my wonderful husband," she replied in a tired but happy voice.

He bent down and placed a gentle kiss on her lips. "I love you. Thank you for our son."

"I love you too. Isn't he beautiful?" she whispered.

"He certainly is," he said.

The midwife took the baby from his arms and made shooing motions, indicating they needed to clean up the bed and his wife. Leaning down, he kissed Selena again and told her he'd be back after he spread the good news to their family and friends.

Gerald found them gathered in the family room around the newly decorated Christmas tree. "We have a healthy boy," he said to cheers and hearty slaps on the back. "We named him William Phillip Lawrence."

"A fine name! You have honored both grandfathers," Banbury said.

"And how is Selena?" Diana asked.

"She's resting, but she's as happy and elated as I am. I'm so proud of her." Just speaking of his wife and the birth gave Gerald a jolt of euphoria. It felt good to release the tension and worry that had tied him into knots over the past several hours.

"I've never known a doctor to let the husband in the room," Percival said. "It must have been an amazing experience to welcome your son into the world."

"It was." Gerald couldn't contain his excitement. "I plan to always be in the room if we are fortunate enough to have more children. Good God, I've never been so scared in all my life—scared for Selena and scared for the baby. And worried I wouldn't be what she needed. It's an experience I will never forget, Percival." He paused and took a deep breath. "If you want to see the baby, Selena should be ready to have visitors in a day or two. I know she'll want to see all of you." Selfishly, he was glad she needed a couple of days of rest—which he planned to spend by her side.

"Congratulations, my friend," Wright said with a wry smile. "I always knew you had it in you. That's a sterling name you've given your son. What will you call him—Phillip or William?"

"My guess is Phillip, but I'm sure Selena already has ideas on that. After all, she did bring him into the world—it's her decision," Gerald said.

He was happy to share the news with everyone, but anxious to get back to Selena and their son. He couldn't wait to hold them again. He spent an hour with his friends and their family while Anna and the other women were making Selena more comfortable. Eventually, the maid came down to let him know that Selena was settled and asking for him. He excused himself and ran up the stairs, taking them two at a time. Stepping into the room, he found his wife and mother-in-law deep in conversation. Thinking he needed to give them privacy, he turned to leave.

"No, Gerald, please stay!" Selena exclaimed. "Maman just gave me some exciting news! Connery has asked her to marry him. They plan to marry on New Year's Day, and they'd like to have Paul and Kat be part of the wedding. They will be so excited to be part of their new grandparents' big day."

Gerald smiled down at his lovely wife. She was blissfully happy. To think, he'd spent years of his life resenting being engaged to her, only to find out marriage to her was the path to happiness.

"Well, that tells me why Connery is suddenly consumed with getting the chapel refurbished. But now that I understand, I'm sure we can hire additional workers to see that it's done quickly," Gerald said.

And they did.

⇥⇥⇥⇤⇤⇤

CHRISTMAS MORNING WAS magical. It was everything Gerald could have wished for, spending a quiet morning with Selena and their new son.

"How many children should we have, my dearest?" he asked.

"We just got through our firstborn's birth, darling. And we've adopted Paul and Kat. I think we'll be busy for a while with three children. Besides, that decision rests with God."

"Of course, but God needs a little help from us, don't you think?" He laughed. "I could see myself enjoying at least one a year for the next five years."

She swatted at him. "One a year! Heavens that would mean I'd be fat for the next five years…"

"I prefer to think of you as voluptuous, my love." He grinned, waggling his brows at her.

Selena promptly blushed. How he loved to make her blush.

"Not in front of Phillip," she gently scolded him, covering their son's perfect little ears as she nursed him.

"Phillip's a newborn. He can't understand what we're saying yet."

"Well, even so, I need a little breathing room in between. Maybe we can agree to two more. That will be five children—some people might believe that it is a large family. What do you think?"

"We can *start* with two more, and then we'll see."

"You're incorrigible." She giggled.

"Only for you, my love."

He watched Selena sing to their son as she continued to nurse him. He would never tire of watching her. Smiling, he reached into his coat pocket and withdrew a long velvet box and one that was ring-sized. "I thought these might be fitting," he said softly.

"Oh, darling, thank you! Please open them for me," she said. He opened the first gift, and she gasped in delight, her eyes filling with tears. "I've never seen a bracelet such as this."

"It's a charm bracelet. You can select charms that symbolize meaningful memories or events in your life. I've selected a pearl with an aquamarine stone in it to symbolize Phillip's birth month. And I've added the opal for Kat and the emerald for Paul. There's a golden document with a diamond in the middle. Known only to us, that's my effort to symbolize the betrothal agreement," he said, grinning. "The beginning of *us* can be traced back to that momentous agreement, and for that, I shall be eternally thankful."

Selena wiped tears from the corners of her eyes. "It's the loveliest bracelet I've ever seen, with such a beautiful sentiment. Thank you."

Gerald opened the second gift and held it up to Selena, who promptly began to cry again. It was a gold band with the children's birthstones surrounding her own. "It's beautiful. I've never had a ring with my birthstone."

"I will add additional birthstones—as we have more children—to it," he said with a grin.

"I love it!"

Gerald slipped it onto her finger and kissed her. "Thank you, love."

Then, a faint flush stained her cheeks. "Gerald, I have nothing to give you..."

He arched a brow. "Are you jesting, my love? You've given me a son...an heir. You've welcomed Paul and Kat into our home as their new mother. I could never ask for more. And you've given me your heart. What more could a man want? I'm the most fortunate of men. Happy Christmas, darling."

THEY DECIDED TO open the rest of the presents after the family had had a late breakfast. By then, Paul and Kat had begun to fidget with excitement.

The children both whooped with joy when Gerald took them out to the stable to meet their new ponies, and they couldn't wait to ride the animals. Dutch took an active role in holding the lead and walking the ponies around the ring outside the stable. The dog had also taken little Phillip into his circle of protection. When he wasn't sitting with Selena or spending time in the nursery watching over her children, he was in the stables, visiting old friends. The dog had become an integral part of their family.

Later that afternoon, Gerald was lifting Selena's feet onto a plump stool in their bedchamber when she tapped him on the head. "Yes, my queen?" he said.

"I think something is brewing between Anna and Percival," she whispered. "She seems to talk about him a lot when she's up here. She even asked me if I thought he was handsome."

"And what did you say?"

"I said he was handsome, but not as handsome as you."

"Good answer," he whispered, leaning down for a kiss. "Now that you mention it, I saw them chatting in the drawing room earlier." He'd observed the newly minted viscount doing his darndest to walk a blushing Anna under the mistletoe.

"They would make a lovely couple, don't you think?" Selena said. "Every time Percival stops by for a visit to supposedly ask your advice about something, he inevitably finds some reason to accidentally bump into Anna."

"You don't say…"

"I do say. I think we might have another wedding within the

year," she whispered.

He sat down next to Selena and kissed her cheek. "Sweet wife, are you planning something?"

She grinned and laid her head on his shoulder. "Oh, just everyone's future…"

About the Author

Anna St. Claire is a big believer that *nothing* is impossible if you believe in yourself. She sprinkles her stories with laughter, romance, mystery and lots of possibilities, adhering to the belief that goodness and love will win the day.

Anna is both an avid reader author of American and British historical romance. She and her husband live in Charlotte, North Carolina with their two dogs and often, their two beautiful granddaughters, who live nearby. *Daughter, sister, wife, mother, and Mimi*—all life roles that Anna St. Claire relishes and feels blessed to still enjoy. And she loves her pets – dogs and cats alike, and often inserts them into her books as secondary characters. And she loves chocolate and popcorn, a definite nod to her need for sweet followed by salty…*but not together*—a tasty weakness!

Anna relocated from New York to the Carolinas as a child. Her mother, a retired English and History teacher, always encouraged Anna's interest in writing, after discovering short stories she would write in her spare time.

As a child, she loved mysteries and checked out every *Encyclopedia Brown* story that came into the school library. Before too long, her fascination with history and reading led her to her first historical romance—Margaret Mitchell's *Gone With The Wind*, now a treasured, but weathered book from being read multiple times. The day she discovered Kathleen Woodiwiss,' books, *Shanna* and *Ashes In The Wind*, Anna became hooked. She read every historical romance that came her way and dreams of writing her own historical romances took seed.

Today, her focus is primarily the Regency and Civil War eras, although Anna enjoys almost any period in American and British history. She would love to connect with any of her readers on her website – www.annastclaire.com, through email – annastclaire author@gmail.com, Instagram – annastclaire_author, BookBub – www.bookbub.com/profile/anna-st-claire, Twitter – @1AnnaSt Claire, Facebook – facebook.com/authorannastclaire or on Amazon – amazon.com/Anna-St-Claire/e/B078WMRHHF.